9/17

SPECIAL MESSAGE TO READERS

THE ULVERSCROFT FOUNDATION
(registered UK charity number 264873)

was established in 1972 to provide funds for
research, diagnosis and treatment of eye diseases.
Examples of major projects funded by
the Ulverscroft Foundation are:-

- The Children's Eye Unit at Moorfields Eye Hospital, London
- The Ulverscroft Children's Eye Unit at Great Ormond Street Hospital for Sick Children
- Funding research into eye diseases and treatment at the Department of Ophthalmology, University of Leicester
- The Ulverscroft Vision Research Group, Institute of Child Health
- Twin operating theatres at the Western Ophthalmic Hospital, London
- The Chair of Ophthalmology at the Royal Australian College of Ophthalmologists

You can help further the work of the Foundation
by making a donation or leaving a legacy.
Every contribution is gratefully received. If you
would like to help support the Foundation or
require further information, please contact:

THE ULVERSCROFT FOUNDATION
The Green, Bradgate Road, Anstey
Leicester LE7 7FU, England
Tel: (0116) 236 4325

website: www.foundation.ulverscroft.com

Jim Shepard is the highly acclaimed author of several novels and short-story collections. He lives in Massachusetts with his family and teaches creative writing at the historical liberal arts establishment Williams College.

Visit his website at:
jimshepard.wordpress.com

THE BOOK OF ARON

My mother and father named me Aron, but my father said they should have named me What Have You Done, and my uncle told everyone they should have called me What Were You Thinking . . . Aron is a nine-year-old Polish Jew, and a born troublemaker. Then, in 1939, the walls go up around the Warsaw Ghetto. As lice and typhus rage, families starve and fight, it is Aron who always finds a way, however dangerous — or treacherous — to survive. But when he is flung together with orphanage director Janusz Korczak, Aron begins to learn of something greater than survival . . .

Books by Jim Shepard
Published by Ulverscroft:

PAPER DOLL

JIM SHEPARD

◆

THE BOOK
OF ARON

Complete and Unabridged

ULVERSCROFT
Leicester

First published in Great Britain in 2015 by
Quercus
London

First Large Print Edition
published 2017
by arrangement with
Quercus Publishing Ltd
An Hachette UK Company
London

A catalogue record for this book is available from the British Library.

ISBN 978-1-4448-3446-8

Published by
F. A. Thorpe (Publishing)
Anstey, Leicestershire

Set by Words & Graphics Ltd.
Anstey, Leicestershire
Printed and bound in Great Britain by
T. J. International Ltd., Padstow, Cornwall

For Ida

A glossary is placed at the back
of this book.

My mother and father named me Aron, but my father said they should have named me What Have You Done, and my uncle told everyone they should have called me What Were You Thinking. I broke medicine bottles by crashing them together and let the neighbors' animals loose from pens. My mother said my father shouldn't beat such a small boy, but my father said that one misfortune was never enough for me, and my uncle told her that my kind of craziness was like stealing from the rest of the family.

When I complained about it my mother reminded me I had only myself to blame, and that in our family the cure for a toothache was to slap the other side of your face. My older brother was always saying we all went without cradles for our backsides or pillows for our heads. Why didn't he complain some more, my mother suggested. Maybe she could light the stove with his complaints.

My uncle was my mother's brother and he was the one who started calling me Sh'maya because I did so many things that made him put his finger to his nose as a warning and

1

say, 'God has heard.' We shared a house with another family in Panevzys near the Lithuanian border. We lived in the front room with a four-paned window and a big stove with a tin sheet on top. Our father was always off looking for money. For a while he sold animal hides. Our mother wished he would do something else, but he always said the pope and the peasant each had their own work. She washed other people's floors and when she left for the day our neighbors did whatever they wanted to us. They stole our food and threw our things into the street. Then she came home exhausted and had to fight with them about how they'd treated us, while I hid behind the rubbish pile in the courtyard. When my older brothers got home they'd be part of the shouting, too. Where's Sh'maya? they'd ask when it was over. I'd still be behind the rubbish pile. When the wind was strong, grit got in my eyes.

Sh'maya only looks out for himself, my uncle always said, but I never wanted to be like that. I lectured myself on walks. I made lists of ways I could improve. Years went by like one unhappy day.

My mother tried to teach me the alphabet, unsuccessfully. She used a big paper chart attached to a board and pointed to a bird or a little man or a purse and then to the letter that went with them. A whole day was spent trying to get me to draw the semicircle and straight line of the letter alef. But I was like something that had been raised in the wild. I didn't know the names of objects. Teachers talked to me and I stared back. Alef, beys, giml, daled, hey, vov, zayin. My last kheyder results before we moved reported my conduct was unsatisfactory, my religion unsatisfactory, my arithmetic unsatisfactory, and even my wood- and metal-shop work unsatisfactory. My father called it the most miserable report he'd ever seen, and invited us all to figure out how I had pulled it off. My mother said that I might've been getting better in some areas and he told her that if God gave me a second or a third life I'd still understand nothing. He said a person with strong character could correct his path and start again but a coward or weakling could not. I always wondered if others had such difficulty in learning. I always worried what would become of me if I couldn't do anything at all. It was terrible to have to be the person I was.

I spent rainy days building dams in the street to divert the runoff. I found boards and pushed them along puddles with sticks. My mother dragged me out of the storms, saying when she found me that there I sat with my dreams full of fish and pancakes. She said while she bundled me into bed next to the stove that I'd never avoided an illness, from chicken pox to measles and scarlet fever to whooping cough, and that was why I'd spent my whole life ninety-nine percent dead.

At night I lay waiting for sleep like our neighbor's dog waited for passing wagons. When she heard me still awake my mother would come to my bedside even as tired as she was. To help me sleep she said that if I squeezed my eyelids tight, lights and planets would float down past them, though I'd never be able to count them before they disappeared. She said that her grandfather told her that God moved those lights and planets with his little finger. I told her I was sorry for the way I was and she said that she wasn't worried about school, only about how I was with my family and our neighbors. She said that too often my tongue worked but not my head, or my head worked but not my heart.

★ ★ ★

Yet when my younger brother was born, I told her I wanted him thrown into the chicken coop. I was glum that whole year, when I was four, because of an infected vaccination on my arm. My mother said I played alone even when other kids were about. Two years went by without my learning a thing. I didn't know how to swim or ride a bicycle, I had no grandparents, no aunts, and no godparents. When I asked why, my father said it was because society's parasites ate well while the worthy received only dirty water, and my mother said it was because of sickness. I attended kheyder until my father came back from one of his trips and told my mother that it was 1936 and time for me to get a modern education. I was happy to change, since our kheyder teacher always had food in his beard and caned us across the fingers for wrong answers and his house smelled like a kennel. So instead I went to a state school, which was cleaner all around. My father was impressed that my new teacher dressed in the European style and that after he taught me to read I started teaching myself. Since I was bored and knew no one I took to books.

And in state school I met my first friend, whose name was Yudl. I liked him. Like me, he had no future. He was always running somewhere with his nose dripping. We made rafts to put in the river and practiced long-distance spitting. He called me Sh'maya too and I called him Pisher. When he wasn't well-behaved he was clever enough to keep the teacher from catching on. One morning before anyone arrived we played tipcat so violently we broke some classroom windows. We scared the boys who had nice satchels and never went barefoot. He was always getting me into trouble at home, and one Sabbath I was beaten for taking apart the family scissors so I could have two little swords, for him and for me. His mother taught him only sad songs, including one about the king of Siberia, before she got sick because of her teeth and died. He came looking for me once she was dead but I hid from him. He told me the next day that two old men carried her out of the house on a board and then his father moved him away.

* * *

That summer a card arrived for my father from his cousin in Warsaw, telling him there was work in his factory. The factory made fabric out of cotton thread. My father hitched a ride to the city in a truck full of geese and then sent for us. He moved us to 21 Zamenhofa Street, Apartment no. 6 — my mother had us each memorize the address so we could find it when we got lost — and my younger brother, who had a bad lung, spent his days at the back window looking out at the rubbish bins. We both thought the best thing about the move was the tailor's shop across the square. The tailor made uniforms for the army and in the front of his window there were three rows of hand-sized mannequins, each dressed in miniature uniforms. We especially loved the tiny service ribbons and medals.

Because it was summer I was expected to work at the factory, so far away that we had to ride the tram. I was shut up in a little room with no windows and four older boys and set to finishing the fabrics. The bolts had to be scraped until they acquired a grain like you found on winter stockings. Each of them took hours and someone as small as me had to lean his chest onto the blade to scrape with enough force. On hot days sweat ran off me like rain off a roof. The other boys said things like, 'What a fine young man from the country we now have in our midst; he's clearly going to be a big wheel in town,' and I thought, am I only here so they can make fun of me? And I refused to go back.

My father said he would give me such a beating that it would hurt to raise my eyebrows, but while I sat there like a mouse under the broom my mother stopped him and said there was plenty I could do at home and school was beginning in a few weeks anyway. My father said I'd only been given a partial hiding and she told him that would do for now, and that night once they started snoring I crept to their beds and kissed her goodnight and pulled the blanket from his feet so that he'd maybe catch a chill.

Because I couldn't sleep I helped her with the day's first chores, and she told everyone she was lucky to have a son who didn't mind rising so early. I worked hard and kept her company. I emptied her wash buckets and fetched hot compresses for my brother's chest. She asked if this wasn't much better than breaking bottles and getting into trouble, and I told her it was, I was still so small that I could squat and ride the bristle block of the long-handled brush she used to polish the floors.

When she told my father at least now their children were better behaved he told her that not one of us looked either well-fed or good-tempered. He joked at dinner that she cooked like a washerwoman. 'Go to a restaurant,' she said in response. She later told me that when she was young she never complained, so her mother would always know who her best child was and keep her near. So I became myself only once the lights went out, and in the mornings went back to pretending things were okay.

At our new school we sat not at one filthy table but on real school benches. I wanted more books but had no money for them and when I tried to borrow them from my classmates they said no. I dealt with bullies by not fighting until the bell for class was about to be rung. When my mother complained to my teacher that a classmate had called me a dirty Jew, my teacher said, 'Well he is, isn't he?' and from then on she made me take weekly baths. I stayed at that school until another teacher twisted a girl's ear until he tore it, and then my mother moved me back to a kheyder where they also taught Polish, two tram stops away. But I still shrank from following instruction like a dog from a stick, My new teacher asked my mother what anyone could do with a kid who was so full of answers. He's like a fox, this one, he said; he's eight going on eighty. And when she reported the meeting to my father he gave me another hiding. That night she came to my bedside and sat and asked me to explain myself and at first I couldn't answer, and then I finally told her that I had figured out that most people didn't understand me and that those who did wouldn't help.

My two older brothers got jobs outside of

town driving goats to the slaughterhouse and were gone until after dark, and like my father they thought my mother should stay at home, so she confided in me about her plan to expand her laundry business. She said it was no gold mine but it could be a serious help, especially before Passover and Rosh Hashanah. She told me she used some of their hidden savings to buy soap and bleach and barrels and that every time my father passed the money's hiding place she had a block of ice under her skull and could feel every hair on her head. I said why shouldn't she take the money, and she was so happy she told me that once I turned nine she would make me a full partner. And this made me happy, because I knew that once I had enough money I would run away to Palestine or Africa.

The week before Passover we set giant pots of water to boil on the stove and we pushed all the bed linens and garments we'd collected from her customers into two barrels with metal rims and she lathered everything with a yellow block of soap before we rinsed it all and ran it through the wringer and dragged all that wet laundry in baskets up to the attic, where she'd strung ropes in every direction under the rafters. Since we opened the windows for the cross-breezes, she couldn't rest that night and whispered to me about the gangs that specialized in crossing rooftops to steal laundry, so I slept up there so that she could relax.

'See? You don't only care about yourself,' she whispered when she came to wake me the next morning. She put her lips to my forehead and her hand to my cheek. When she touched me like that, it was as if the person everyone hated had flown away. And while he was gone, I didn't let her know that I was already awake.

★ ★ ★

I didn't need to play with anyone, so after school I came home and helped her instead. While my younger brother napped, we talked about our days. I told her about a soldier on a horse near the tram stop on Gęsia who took some coins from his saddlebag and handed them to me, and she asked if I'd thanked him and of course I hadn't. She agreed it was a strange thing he'd done and wondered if he'd been thinking of his own little boy. We listened to our neighbors arguing across the hall, and she said the father spent his days in the synagogue securing himself a place in the next world while the mother wore herself out seeing that everyone was fed. She said that the mother had had fourteen children and only six had survived. I said maybe they were finished having children, and she said that for the mother's sake, may a six-winged angel descend with the news.

I did kindnesses for my mother but she always wanted me to do them instead for my little brother. He was afraid of everything. She kept a lit candle near his bed to drive shadows out of corners because his window had no shutters and at night he always thought someone was standing beside it outside or knocking on the wall, and he cried himself to sleep about it. When she went to comfort him his eyes were so full of fear it scared me to look at them. Our father shouted at him to stop, which made things worse. He reminded my brother that everyone in the building understood that parents didn't need to hold back and could give rule-breakers what they deserved. He'd work himself up about it and then our mother would placate him in the other room after telling me to stay with my brother and do what I could to quiet him down.

My brother had all sorts of medicines and drops and inhaler-pots on his bedside table and my mother taught us how to grab his head and tilt it forward when he had trouble breathing and started to choke. He hated being inside all the time and finally ran away and left a note saying he'd had enough of this life, and he was missing for two days. Once he was back my mother locked him in the apartment and he pulled his chair to the window so he could see outside.

I didn't understand him but liked the blank way he didn't complain. He cupped any treat he was given in his hands and peeked at it before passing it along to one of us. If he wasn't napping or staring out his window, he stayed near my mother. When he got angry he didn't hit anyone or shout but instead went for days without speaking. My mother had a saying about how quiet he got, that his wisdom died inside of him, something her own mother had said about her. She told the neighbors that as a toddler he'd once laid himself spread-eagled on the tram tracks to prevent her from leaving, and she'd had to carry him home, and that when she asked him about it afterwards he'd put his hands over her mouth.

* * *

He loved the radio and it was because of him that I first heard Janusz Korczak's show. Thursday afternoons I had to sit with him and we could hear it through the wall, since our neighbor's wife was hard of hearing. The show was called *The Old Doctor* and I liked it because even though he complained about how alone he was, he always wanted to know more about other people, especially kids. I also liked that I never knew what to expect. Sometimes he interviewed poor orphans in a summer camp. Other times he talked about what he loved about airplanes. Or told a fairy tale. He made his own barnyard noises. When I asked my mother why the show was called *The Old Doctor* she said there'd been complaints about allowing a Jewish educator to shape the minds of Polish children.

That was also the year I first ate in a restaurant. My father took me to celebrate some good fortune he never explained. It was the first time I was able to choose my own food. He quizzed me on Jan Henryk Dąbrowski while I ate since he considered himself an amateur historian. While I was eating dessert he made me laugh by breaking walnuts with his teeth. That night I dreamed that a raven was sitting on my shoulder in the wind and a black cloak was streaming out behind me. When my father was getting dressed the next morning I put my arms around him. 'What's the matter with him today?' he asked my mother before he left.

* ★ ★ ★

The kids on my street reacted to my lack of interest with their own. Sometimes they threw stones at me. Another whole summer came and went. I wanted to learn how to ride a bicycle, so I went to a boy who owned one and he said he would teach me. I could get on by myself after the first lesson but then he wouldn't teach me anymore. I met Lutek one evening when I sat near some kids I didn't know and they told me to leave but I didn't. He had a rabbit-skin cap with earflaps and when one of the kids asked where he got it he said that he'd found it between the kid's mother's legs, so they started pushing him around. They knocked him into me, so I shoved the kid who'd done it and he landed on his back and head on the paving stones. The other kids chased us and Lutek led me into a cellarway hidden by a coal chute and they all ran by. I asked how he'd found it and he said he'd been hiding since before I was born. While we sat there in the dark I asked him more questions but he stopped answering and just sniffed at the air like a dog.

He was even smaller than me. He was so small he said he had a younger sister who everyone thought was older. He said the village he was from was pitiful. It didn't appear on maps and it was just three lanes of cottages, fences, and mud. He'd gone to school for a year at one at the Talmud-toyres on Mila Street, which he said was famous for graduating ignoramuses. He said his father was the strongest porter in the city and pulled a handcart he harnessed to himself like a horse, He was especially good with the huge machinery crates from Lódz that three men had trouble budging. Otherwise he sat in a tavern. He worked at the railroad station near Jaruszewski's courtyard. That neighborhood scared me. Smoke from the slag heaps always darkened the air over the loading docks.

My mother was happy I'd made a friend but soon upset that I was never around to watch my younger brother once Lutek took charge of my education. He showed me how to steal from the vegetable carts, and how one of us by making a commotion could hide what the other was doing, even when the peddlers were watching out for one another. With a French pamphlet he took from a bookstall he proved I didn't know anything about girls, and discovered I knew so little that I didn't even know what he was talking about. After he had cursed some filthy Russians he also said I didn't know anything about politics, which was also true.

He taught me that no one else's problems

should get in the way of our having a good time. I told him about all the trouble I'd got into with Yudl, including the broken school windows, but he was unimpressed. His family had moved three times since coming to Warsaw and in one neighborhood he'd been hauled in by the police for breaking down the door of a boy who'd stolen his cap, and in another for having put a hole in a kid's head with a jeweler's hammer. He said the kid was okay after a while, though he'd had to wear a head-bandage and everyone had called him the Sheik.

I asked if his father beat him for such offenses and he said he'd had more luck with his father's strap since he'd learned to rub garlic and onion onto the welts. And that he was lucky that his father was more upset about his sister's stutter. His father tried to cure it by mimicking her, to shame her into getting over it. She liked me because when I had to wait for her to finish what she was saying I never got impatient. She told Lutek that I was kind and he should bring me around more often, so he had me talk to her while he slipped money from her secret hiding-spot. He said she knew he stole from her but she never complained about it. When he took enough we would buy sausages and ride the tram.

On those days I was around and my younger brother was feeling better my mother ordered me to take him to the park so he could get some fresh air. He was always thrilled to go. The back courtyard with the rubbish bins got no light and was deserted except for the occasional stray cat, Lutek always found us wherever we went. He said that being saddled with a consumptive wasn't the end of the world and we could always find some uses for him, so one day we persuaded him to steal a jar of jam and on another to sing to a policeman. Or else we went about our business and he followed along. Whenever Lutek saw his blank look he asked him, 'So how's the weather in Wilno?' a joke my younger brother never understood.

On our way home I told him not to tell our mother about whatever we had done, and then she said he had to, and so he did, and I wouldn't get supper that night. Then after he went to sleep she would sit at the foot of my bed and we'd look at each other. Neither of us would speak until she finally asked me to try to remain a decent human being and then kissed my cheek before wishing me a good night. And I would look up at my ceiling in the darkness and remember that I gave her nothing in return for what she gave me, and almost never had. Then I would plan my next day with Lutek.

★   ★   ★

She gave me a party for my ninth birthday, the day after the party Lutek's sister asked how it had been, and he said what was there to tell about it. We had raisin cake and the guests were my younger brother and Lutek. My younger brother gave me a book of his drawings and my mother sewed me a leather satchel.

That whole winter my younger brother's health improved until it got worse and he had to go to the hospital. Before he got sick my mother had pneumonia and took to her bed for a week, and he spent the whole time on the end of her blanket, staring. When she woke up she would ask me to get him a sweater and I'd ask if he was cold and he would say no. He was starting to cough too, and she finally got out of bed to drape a muffler around his neck. Then after she said she was feeling better he got so excited he ran around the back courtyard in a rainstorm and came in soaked and shaking.

For a while she tried to take care of him herself at home. She had me read to him in the afternoons, and he always chose a book called *Jur* about two brothers, one sickly and in constant need of looking after and the other a picture of health who ended up dying. My younger brother always liked the end in particular, when the sickly brother stood over the healthy brother's grave and talked about how much he missed him.

Finally it turned out that he had pneumonia too and had to go to the hospital. By then he had to be carried through the streets in an ambulance.

My mother and I sat with him when we could. My older brothers and father visited once, all together. They brought him a big tin of sweets that they opened and sampled.

He hated being left at the hospital at night and screamed at our leaving. My mother always wept all the way home. After three days his fever was so high he didn't recognize us. The nurses brought him compresses but he was so hot they couldn't keep them cold. They brought him bread soaked in milk and we helped him open his mouth to eat it.

The day he died I told him that he was acting like an older boy, being brave. My mother had brought him home and he said he wished he could buy me the tailor shop's miniature uniform of the Uhlans Regiment, which was my favorite. My mother was at the pharmacy and he asked when she was coming back. He said she'd been telling him how much better he was getting, but that now she sounded less sure. He breathed like someone was sitting on his chest, and it was hard for him to say even that much.

When my mother returned she found him out of bed and standing in his nightshirt on a chair to look out his window. She warmed his feet and got him back into bed and told him that if he looked outside when he woke, then all of his dreams would escape. She sent me to the kitchen to make him some tea and asked if I thought I could do that much. While I was filling the kettle I could see them both. She took his hands and called for him to look at her. She said she wanted to tell him a story, that it was going to be a long story, and he needed to stay awake for it. He seemed to come out of a daze and smiled at her. The story was about a poor Jew and a sultan. She said about one of the sultan's decisions, 'Isn't that amazing?' and while she was asking him, he died.

★   ★   ★

She stayed in bed for two weeks. I did what housework I could. My father and brothers ate at taverns. I made my own dinners. Lutek stayed away. Once the sun had set my mother took to talking to me in the dark. She wouldn't let me light any lamps until my father and brothers came home. After my brothers went to sleep, my father would sit up at the kitchen table with vodka and weep without making any noise.

She said she forgave me. She said none of us had done all we could for my younger brother. She said she still remembered when she'd been a little girl and a teacher had said, 'I predict that someday you are really going to amount to something.' She said this teacher had told her favorite students, 'Well, you're sitting on the wagon. Let's see how far you can travel down the road.' She said this teacher had awarded her with a book inscribed *For your good conduct and many talents*.

She said she'd lost all of her energy for work, but that maybe it would return in time. She said her feelings were like a coin in a strongbox and that from now on maybe I alone would have the key. She said she knew that my father was spending what little money they had saved. Let him take it and choke on it, she said. Maybe then he'd leave her in peace.

She said that when she was ten she'd had to care for her infant sister, who screamed when she was wet, screamed when she was hungry, and screamed when she was poorly diapered. She said she used to run all over the house holding her sister, not knowing what her sister wanted from her. She said she'd lived for the day when her mother would come home and take her sister back, and everyone would be happy with the good work she had done.

When it got warmer, she started cooking again and doing a little cleaning. She went outside. My tenth birthday came and went without raisin cake. One morning when I thanked her for my breakfast she said that the older she got, the more of an infant she became. I asked if she was feeling better and if she wanted to walk in the park when I got home from school, and she said that yes, she did. She said that sometimes it felt as if everything had been taken from her, and that all she wanted was to take something back.

★ ★ ★

The next morning my father told me to get up because it was war and the Germans had invaded. I didn't believe him, so he pointed at the neighbors' apartment and said, 'Come to the radio, you'll hear it.'

People had spent the day before taping up

windows and running through the streets buying up food. In the morning our teacher told us that as of the next day our school, which had had an anti-aircraft battery moved onto its roof, was under military control, that we should leave our registration books to be signed, and that he would see us after the war. We wanted to go to the roof to view the anti-aircraft guns but a soldier wouldn't let us on the staircase.

When I got home, my father and older brothers were taping our windows and one of my brothers showed me a blue glass filter that would fit over our flashlight.

That afternoon we saw an airplane with smoke coming out of its tail and two others chasing after it. Another plane flew over very low and a soldier took his rifle and started shooting at it until people on the street screamed that he was endangering everyone, so he stopped.

There were air raid sirens at night but for a few weeks nothing happened. Lutek would tell me the next day how much he liked the sirens because everyone had to get out of bed whatever time it was and the kids in his building would meet in the basement and play. He said all of the kids in his building liked the air raids except one whose mother was crazy and caused a lot of trouble by running out into the street and uncovering the windows while the sirens were still going.

For a few days in the afternoons we went to our neighbors' apartment to hear the news. It was all bad.

The bombardment of the city lasted all day and night without stopping and went on into the next day and night. We stayed in the cellar and the wailing and crying and praying drowned out the explosions if they were far away. My mother sat against the wall with her arms around me and whenever I stood to stretch my legs she asked where I was going. My father and brothers sat against the opposite wall. After three days things quieted and someone came down the stairs and shouted that Warsaw had surrendered. My mother told us not to leave but my brothers and I climbed out into the street.

Dust and soot hung in the air. There were giant craters in the intersection. The big tree on the corner had flown all apart. Our back courtyard was covered with broken glass. Down Gęsia Street something was still burning.

My mother led us back up to our apartment, which only had some broken windows. She sent us out to look for planks to board them up, so I walked over to Lutek's neighborhood. He threw his arm around me and grinned and said, 'Well, we survived the war.' I told him what we were looking for and he led me to an alley fence that was blown apart. Together we brought home so many planks that my father told my mother to leave me alone whenever I wanted to go out during the day. We especially needed water since nothing came out of our taps, and Lutek showed me how to steal from his building's cistern.

We gathered anything we might need. Sometimes we were chased off, but not often. The destroyed buildings were a great playground and we always found something surprising in the rubble. One building's entire front had been sheared away and we could see into every apartment up to the roof, and near the top a family was still living there. They looked like a store display. One leg of an iron bedstead hung out into space. In the attic, sparrows flew in and out of the holes made by the artillery shells.

On the way home with my water I was stopped by a bald-headed man in a filthy green surgical apron who was carrying a little boy. The man had spectacles covered in dust and a yellowish goatee. 'Where's the shoe store that was here?' he asked.

'There,' I told him, and pointed.

He looked at the smashed walls that had

fallen in on one another. 'I just found him in the street,' he said. The boy looked asleep. 'He can't walk on all this glass without shoes. I have to carry him until I find something for his feet.'

I recognized his voice and said, 'You're the Old Doctor from the radio.'

'Would you have shoes at your house that might fit him?' he said. But then someone else called, 'Pan Doctor! Pan Doctor!' and he turned and carried the boy off in that direction.

★ ★ ★

When the Germans marched in, the crowds were so quiet I could hear a fly that was bothering a woman a few feet away. Lutek said there was more noise at the parade on his street and that some people waved little flags with swastikas on them. At the market square the next day no vegetable stalls were set up and instead more Germans unloaded crates from trucks. One talked to me in Polish. 'Bring us something to drink,' he told me, and then he and his friends straddled the crates and waited.

Later that week they set up a soup kitchen and handed out free bread. The soldiers seemed to never be sure where they wanted everyone to line up. They enjoyed herding people from place to place. A little girl with big ears waited three hours in line with us and when she got her soup she handed it to Lutek and said she wasn't hungry. After she left he told me she was a neighbor and that her parents and sister had been buried in their building during the bombardment. He said that when you saw the building you knew they wouldn't be dug out until Christmas.

That night two Germans showed up at our door looking for furniture. They roamed around our apartment before deciding we had nothing they liked. They went next door to our neighbors with the radio and took two chairs and a soup tureen. The husband told us after they left that they'd pulled him around by the nose with pliers because he hadn't said a courteous enough hello.

The next day the Polish police had taken over the soup kitchen and the soldiers were gone. Then the day after that the Polish police were gone and so was the soup kitchen.

★　★　★

That winter we did all of our scrounging in heavy rain. Streets were like marshes because of the big dirty puddles between the cobblestones. We had to be careful because everything was extra slippery. It didn't help that in January Jews could no longer be on the streets after nine and before five. Lutek's father sometimes had to leave his crate where it was and get it in the morning. Most were so heavy that no one could steal them anyway. He told us about one of the other porters who claimed that because he was so ugly the Germans constantly interrupted his work to take pictures of him.

All Jews had to wear yellow armbands, Lutek said that the extra layer would help keep us warm.

There was always a new rule. My mother was upset about the one that made Jews show a delousing certificate to ride the trams. Then she was upset that we could no longer ride certain trams. Then she was upset that we had to declare our possessions and said it would be the first step in stripping us of everything we had. My father reminded her that the Germans had already been in our apartment and had found nothing worth taking.

Lutek and I rode whatever trams we wanted because he taught me how to wear a half-sleeve over a long-sleeved shirt so we could roll it down to cover our armbands. And he showed me how you had to jump off if the tram drivers slowed in a certain way because it meant that Germans were waiting at the next stop. Once we jumped off right into some German police but they only took us by the collars and told us to help a doctor who was being made to empty all of the silver from his sideboard into some waiting cars. The doctor kept asking us to be careful with everything. After the last load he asked a German if he could keep his grandmother's saltcellar, a little boat he showed us, because it had great sentimental value for him, and the German said no.

'Who leaves so many things lying around?' my mother asked at dinner about the loot I brought home, and my father said what did she know about it, that she should be quiet and count her blessings.

'It's a blessing he's safe and I want to keep him that way,' she told him.

'Does he look like he'd do anything dangerous?' he said.

Lutek agreed this really was the best thing about me; that I didn't. We specialized in pantry and bathroom windows that you wouldn't think a cat could fit through. I'd give him a boost and then wait at the end of the alley for his whistle. If all was clear I'd whistle back and he'd dump whatever he'd found down to me and off I'd go, to meet up with him later on.

When it came to tools he had an eye for things you couldn't find a use for at first. He lifted a thick short wire off the flatbed of a truck and it turned out to be perfect for working through a sash and casement, because once it was through it was rigid enough that you could tap the hook until it popped from the eyelet.

He had found someone who would trade most of what we got for most of what we wanted, so some days I'd bring my mother coal and some days flour and some days something else. One night I brought home almonds, but it didn't matter because some women in fur coats had been ordered to wash the pavement with their underwear and then to put the underwear back on again, wet, and my mother and everyone else had been forced to watch, and she was still upset.

I told Lutek about it and he told me about having come across an old Jew atop a barrel with some German soldiers cutting his hair, with a crowd gathered around laughing. He said all they were doing was cutting his hair and he couldn't tell how upset the old Jew was, but that he'd told himself then and there he would never let himself end up on top of that barrel. So whatever else happened to him he could always say to himself, well, you're not on top of that barrel.

31

We celebrated our big talk by stealing two expensive fountain-pen sets from a shop and hid them under our shirts while we waited for the tram. The tram was only two blocks away but it hadn't moved for ten minutes and men were standing around the front of it.

We debated whether or not just to walk home. My shoes no longer fitted and my blisters had broken, so I argued we should wait.

There was a girl sitting next to us and Lutek asked her who she was looking at. She asked him who he was looking at. 'What kind of hat do you call that?' she asked.

He told her to go screw herself with an onion. An onion would be better than him, she said. Then she said those were Lamy pens we thought we were hiding. She recognized the cases.

I buttoned my top button and Lutek rubbed his eyes.

She suggested we take them to Siekierska's in Wilanów. She explained when we didn't answer that no one else would buy such expensive pens.

'Let's just walk,' Lutek told me, and then stood up. When I hesitated he went off without me.

I stayed beside the girl for another few minutes. 'Your friend Rabbit Hat doesn't take chances,' she said.

I asked what she thought had happened with the tram and she said it was a good question. I told her my name was Aron and she said she hadn't asked. I asked what her name was and she said Zofia, then turned and looked at me and shook my hand. I asked where she'd gone to school and she said over on Third of May Avenue. She said she'd been picked on as the only Jewish girl. 1 said she didn't look Jewish. She had light hair and a small nose. She thanked me and then said that I did.

She asked if I knew Mańka Lipszyc, and I said yes. She asked if I was the one whose brother had just died and then was quiet at my answer.

The tram never came. She told me she had a younger brother named Leon and an older brother Jechiel and a younger sister Salcia who was only ten months old.

She knew about the pens because her father had owned a stationery store. People came from all over the city for the quality of his paper. He supported their family, their grandmother, the unmarried Brysz girls, their Uncle Ickowicz, and Hanka Nasielska and her parents. For a while her family had so much money that she'd gone to the land of preschool where you paid tuition. Her father had a sister in America who begged him to emigrate but he told her that he'd stay where he was in order to mind the shop.

After the Germans arrived they beat him severely and smashed around their apartment hunting for gold. They ended up taking only five meters of dress material from her mother. Even so, her family had been luckier than friends across the street who'd been thrown out of their house and told that their kind of people had slept far too long on soft beds. But then a week after that an SS officer stopped by the shop and was so impressed that he'd instructed her father to arrange to transport the shop's entire stock back to the officer's hometown. Her father had been given a receipt.

They'd lived on Żelazna Street in a big apartment but they'd since had to move and their new neighborhood was so backward that some of the streets weren't even paved and so muddy there were wooden footbridges to the front doors. She said it was sad to watch her mother wade through the mud. She said that her mother had wept for three days and her father had assured them they'd move again soon, that he'd told them that he was starting a broom factory and that the Germans were very fond of brooms.

She said her brother had told her that even

before she was born their parents had been to the rabbi twice for a divorce, that her grandmother had insisted on the marriage and told anyone who would listen that her daughter had married an educated man.

I told her I should get going. 'Don't let me keep you,' she said.

But after I didn't get up she said she remembered thinking to herself that maybe their family's move would change everything, even her, and things wouldn't be so bad. She said the years before school that she couldn't remember had probably been the happiest of her life. I didn't know what to answer. Finally she stood up and stretched and said she was late. Then she bent down with her hands on her thighs and said that if I carried the pen case under my belt in the back it might be harder to spot.

* * *

Work on the walls began as soon as it got warmer. My mother at first celebrated the news that the Judenrat had been ordered to quarantine the Jews who were sick. Then she realized we might be part of the area to be sealed off. She went with our neighbors to report there was no typhus in our building, but that only meant she spent days waiting to talk to an official who wouldn't listen and couldn't do anything.

All day long outside our window we heard wheelbarrows squeaking and trowels scraping and the clink of bricks. It started and stopped, so for days there might be just a few rows and then suddenly something you couldn't see over. As far as Lutek was concerned, for the time being it was another opportunity. After the workers quit for the day at a dead end near Niska, we carried off two big bags of cement.

In the evenings my brothers argued about what was happening. I had other things to worry about. Whenever there was big news our neighbors with the radio knocked on our door. Holland and Belgium and Luxembourg had all been invaded, I asked Lutek if he thought Belgium would surrender and he said that it didn't matter, since the way things went for us either one bad thing or another would happen.

No one wanted linens or floors washed anymore, so what I brought home was more important than ever.

In May it got warm and we worked later. Lutek and I got into a scrape, so I ducked into an entryway and waited and was about to leave it when Zofia took my sleeve. She gestured with her head and we stood there quietly as the shopkeeper and his sons passed by. One had a mallet and the other two had nightsticks, Lutek was somewhere on the other side of the street and might have been long gone. The shopkeeper stopped on the corner in a dry spot and his sons started searching door by door.

'I think you'd better come to dinner,' Zofia whispered into my ear. She was watching through the entryway's frosted glass with me, her cheek close to mine. 'We're right upstairs. You can bring what you have there as your gift.'

Her parents were polite and pleased by the honey, and her mother told their baby it was rare and expensive. They introduced me to her older brother Jechiel, a yeshiva student. He seemed to think I was standing too close to his sister. He said that for looking too often at a woman one was hung by the eyebrows in Hell. Zofia laughed and told me that because his morning prayer, 'Let our days be multiplied,' sounded like 'cheap fish,' it had become his family nickname.

She introduced me to her younger brother, Leon, who seemed unhappy and had little to say. His brother talked about him as if he wasn't in the room, then said that while their parents had hopes for him he'd turned out to be a real dunce, already kept back a grade twice before school had been suspended. Now getting his certificate was going to be like making it to the North Pole at a snail's pace.

Zofia's mother made what she said was a hometown dish, a pudding of buckwheat meal sautéed with onions. She fed it in spoonfuls to the baby, Salcia, who was wedged into a high chair beside her.

Someone rang the bell and Zofia answered the door and stepped out into the hall and talked in a low voice before returning to the table. When her father asked about it she said that the shopkeeper Lebyl was looking for a thief.

They asked about my family and since I had nothing to say I told them about Lutek. I told them that he liked to climb utility poles just to look down on people. I told them that on crowded trams he liked to recite details about what happened between a man and a woman. Zofia's brother was appalled but her father found it funny. She asked if Lutek had ever had a girlfriend and I told her there'd been a girl he admired and that he'd waited every evening for an entire month beside her gate with a letter explaining his feelings but that whenever she came out he'd panic and walk away.

Her father talked about the broom factory

and where the money for it would come from. He talked about Zofia's grandfather, who had never heard a kind word from anyone and at the age of ten had been sent away every night to eat his evening meal at another family's house, and once he had his own children he always preferred scrimping on the family's food to working harder. He said he thought that Zofia took after him. She said she agreed and that as a rule she disliked everyone. He told about how he'd had to throw her out of his shop when she was six years old and had ventured the opinion in front of one of his biggest customers that the price he'd quoted was far too high.

Salcia didn't like the pudding, so her mother cleaned it from her face with a spoon and then offered it to her again and asked if this Lutek I was describing was despite all of that a good boy. I said yes and Zofia said no. Her father laughed and her mother made a face. They never looked at each other but still the family seemed to get by.

It got quiet. Jechiel looked at me as though I was missing something, Zofia's father reminded me about the curfew and her mother thanked me again for the honey, which she hadn't served. Zofia showed me to the door and I didn't know what to make of her look before she closed it and left me in the hall. I told myself as I went down the stairs that there was nothing wrong with having friends, but that there'd be no butting in where I wasn't wanted.

* * *

Everyone in my family was excited about the news that the Germans were fighting in France, and then miserable about the news that the Germans had taken Paris. One of my brothers said it was because they had an airplane that converted to a tank when it set down on the battlefield. My other brother said it was because they had something called a heavy air bomb that surrounded their parachutists with a shield that no bullet could penetrate. My mother said that one believed this and the other believed that but what was fated to happen always will. My father said that one way or another the joke he'd heard at his cousin's factory was that thousands of hammers had arrived from America to pound dreams of salvation out of our heads.

When it was finished the wall was three meters high with another meter of barbed wire on top. I still helped my mother with her chores and each morning she went out to look at it. I asked if she was hoping to find it taken down. They built a wooden bridge across Chłodna Street near St Karol's Church to connect the two ghettos that were separated by the street and tramline. Farther down a gate sealed off Żelazna and all the traffic stopped so the tram could run through.

And now there was typhus in the building across the street. Packages were left on the pavement outside the front entrance because the porters refused to carry them inside.

My mother and father fought more about what I was doing. He said having a macher at a time like this wasn't such a bad thing and she said the big macher was dragging the little macher around on a string. He said she didn't complain when the soup was hot in front of her and she said I was going to get killed or bring the typhus home.

Every morning she searched my clothes for lice and doused my head over the sink with kerosene. She rubbed my neck and behind my ears with a kerosene-soaked rag and scrubbed at my scalp like my hair was the problem. She reminded me she had thought we were partners. I told her that hadn't changed. So where was her partner, she wanted to know. Her partner was off at his own business, I told her.

She rinsed and toweled my head and I got my satchel. Later I felt guilty and told her we could work together all day tomorrow but she told me she'd already learned not to get attached to anything, She asked if I missed my younger brother. She said that if she hadn't been self-centered she wouldn't have survived either. I repeated that we could spend the whole next day together and she said that the day after that we could visit the Promised Land, where everyone ate figs and honey and fish with noodle soup.

* ★ ★

Notices were hung over the gates to the ghetto warning that it was threatened by an epidemic. My mother and father stopped visiting neighborhoods outside the walls and asked me to do the same. I told them I would and went on doing whatever I wanted wherever I wanted to. My mother said that seven people had died across the street, including Mrs Lederman and the Globus twins, and wondered if we were just going to be walled in with all the sick people until everyone was dead. My brother said he'd heard that after the peace the Jews would all be sent to Madagascar, and my mother asked what we would all do in Madagascar. 'Let's get there, first, and then we'll find out,' my father told her.

A week later she heard from the woman who sold her soap that all Jews were to be expelled from the streets crossing Ujazdowskie Avenue and the area adjoining the Vistula. My father asked why we should believe her and my mother reminded him that the woman was Czerniaków's sister-in-law. Two days later he read the same news aloud to us from the paper, as though we'd been arguing with him. Jewish residents in the German quarter had to move out immediately; those in the Polish district could remain for the time being; and all new Jews arriving in the city had to go straight to the walled Jewish district.

Where were they going to put everyone, my brother wanted to know.

'I think they believe that's our problem,' my father told him.

Lutek reported the next day that his father and the rest of the porters had been told it would soon be forbidden in our district to rent to Aryans, and that Christian families were already negotiating to exchange apartments with Jews from other parts of the city. 'So?' I said, and Lutek said, 'You're an idiot,' and that we would have a field day what with all the carts and wagons going back and forth, and he was right.

Proclamations kept appearing in the newspapers and my father kept reading them to the family, always first announcing, 'And under the heading of Things Get Worse . . . ' Each proclamation listed new streets that were to be cleansed of Jews. Pages advertised Aryan-owned apartments inside the walls to be traded for Jewish-owned ones on the outside. Finally in October all Jews were given two weeks to move into the district and told that it had been shrunk by an additional six streets, which meant that those who had already exchanged apartments to get onto those streets now had to exchange apartments again. This was necessary to protect the health and well-being of the soldiers and the general population.

The result was like the worst street bazaar of all time combined with an evacuation. Every road we looked down was a sea of heads and all we heard was a terrible clamor and shouting. Lutek and I spent most of our time at the Leszno Street gate. Jews were hauling overloaded pushcarts and wagons in while Poles tried to haul the same out and the arguments about who could proceed and who had to wait meant that it took hours to get anywhere. Collisions spilled tables and chairs and stoves and pans onto the cobblestones, and half a family's load got snatched away before they could reassemble the other half. Lutek and I rode the crowds up to the wagons and carried off whatever we could. Sometimes kids or old people on the wagons saw what we were doing and shouted to those in front, but in the crush the fathers or older kids could never get to us in time. I got a mantel clock and Lutek pulled away a whole oriental rug. The German and Polish police ignored the Polish carts but grabbed anything they wanted off the Jewish ones. One of the Jews complained, so they overturned his.

On some of the narrower streets pushcart owners who hadn't found apartments went from house to house calling up to the windows to ask if there were any spare rooms. Anyone who had a cart charged whatever he liked, and everyone was a porter, so Lutek's father and the others made money by taking over the pavements in front of their buildings. People moving in unloaded feather beds and laundry baskets but the porters threw them over the fences into the courtyards and the families had to pay to get them back. On every street, children were lost and crying and milling around. Everything Lutek and I carried off we stored in the cellar of his father's building, alongside what his father had collected.

We were separated the day before the deadline and I was knocked to the pavement trying to get closer to a cart. I crawled to the

45

entryway of a building and tried to get my breath back. A kid jerked at my satchel while I was crawling and I kicked at him and drove him away. I lost my balance getting back on my feet and almost put my hand on an SS officer. He and three of his men were watching a Polish policeman whose papers had fallen out of his leather pouch. The policeman was in the road shouting for the crowds to go around him but every time he crouched his pouch slid down off his shoulder and spilled more paper. The SS officer laughed with his men about it. Even I could see that they were afraid of him. His hairline under his cap stopped high on the back of his neck and there was something about the stubble that looked dangerous.

My knees still hurt from where I'd fallen and I put my hands on them. The officer did the same, and his men noticed and smiled. He squinted at me as though he'd said something funny and then straightened up and gestured to his men and they left, one of them looking back and winking before the crowd swallowed them up.

* * *

On the day of the deadline Lutek and I spotted a wagon filled with magical loot — a gilded birdcage, a set of knives in a sunburst pattern in an open display case — and followed it until we had to give up because the crowds were so impossible. Lutek got mad and climbed a lamppost to search out other opportunities while I hung on to it below him. Then we heard a fanfare of horns and pie pans and the gates of the courtyard opposite us opened, and two old caretakers somehow managed to part the mob on the street and a row of kids with horns and tin pans and wooden spoons turned onto the street in a line. A boy in the center held a staff with a bright-green flag and a Jewish star in a harness around his waist. More lines came out of the darkness behind them, kids of all sizes holding toys and books against their chests and singing.

'What is it?' Lutek asked. We couldn't hear what they were singing but the kids kept coming, at least twenty rows of them, followed by wagons piled high with wicker baskets tied with cords and cast-iron pots and floured breadboards and trunks tied with rope, crates of books and ladles and strainers, and then a wagon mounded with coal and another with potatoes. Other kids and adults wrestled over the coal and potatoes that scattered onto the cobblestones when the wagons turned onto the street. All of the

47

wagons had red geraniums in window boxes along their sides, and beneath them decorations made from streamers. The wagon drivers were wearing homemade bird masks with plumes and feathers. We pushed closer and heard someone say it was Korczak's orphanage that had been forced to move. And then there he was with his bald head and yellowish goatee again, the last one out before the courtyard gates swung shut behind him. He was pulling a heavy woman along by the arm and struggling to keep up with the last wagon. She was as tall as he was and seemed more frightened by the crowds.

They were pushed into our path and for a while we were carried along behind them. I wondered if he would recognize me but he didn't. He and the heavy woman had to shout at each other to be heard. She asked how long he thought he could go without sleeping and he shouted back that when he was a young man his mother had come into his room in the mid-afternoon and dragged him out of bed by his feet. 'She asked if that was how I wanted to become a doctor,' he shouted. 'By staying out all night long. And I told her, 'A *doctor*? I thought I was studying to become a lush.''

We followed them to the gate of the small ghetto at Chłodna, where the German and

Polish police were checking identification. All of the orphanage wagons had passed through except the one with the potatoes, which sat still next to the guard hut. The driver had his hands on his hips and was watching two Polish policemen unhitch his horse. He'd pulled his bird mask down and it hung below his chin. A feather fluttered alongside his ear.

'What's happening?' Korczak asked the Polish policeman in front of us. 'Why has my wagon not gone through?'

'This isn't your wagon,' one of the German policemen told him. 'It's my wagon.'

They argued in German about it. The heavy woman was terrified and tried to pull Korczak through the gate but he knocked her arm away. He shouted something at the German and then repeated it to the Polish policeman: that if the German didn't release the potatoes he would report the theft to their superiors. The German's bored expression disappeared and he said in Polish, 'So you're trying to frighten me, Jew?' and Lutek gave my shirt such a pull from behind that he ripped it.

'Are you with him?' a Polish policeman said, stepping in front of us. He pointed a baton at Korczak. 'Is he drunk?'

'I don't know what he is,' I told him, and Lutek pulled me again, and a woman with a chicken in a straw cage shouldered forward and almost knocked the policeman off his feet. He clubbed her once and then twice and Lutek shouted into my ear, 'What do you think this is? A *show*?' and yanked me so hard that I fell to my knees, and then he pulled me to my feet and dragged me down the street.

Families squatted in the halls and fought over pavements. One took over our stairwell near the top floor. They aired out their clothes and bedding on the railings. No one had said the ghetto would be closed and the markets outside the walls declared illegal. There were long lines in front of the food shops and everything was bought up. Our family of course wasn't prepared and hadn't saved any money. Two other families moved in with our neighbors across the hall and my mother said it was only a matter of time before someone moved in with us. When she complained about it my father reminded her that the Christian who owned the building had lived here thirty-seven years and then had to leave nearly all of her furniture behind. He cheered himself by reading the German casualty lists in the newspaper. He called it his Happy Corner. He also paid ten groszy extra for a German paper that showed photos of their cities after Allied bombing.

The small ghetto across Chłodna we heard had attracted the well-to-do Jews and was less crowded. Our neighbor told us that across the hall they were nine to a room. The family on our stairwell took in some extra relatives and bartered old clothes and saccharine on the street in front of our building and screamed and fought in the middle of the night. In the mornings we had to step over them when going down the stairs.

My parents fought too. My mother said we were living like castaways and the apartment was filthy and my father said if we didn't have money for bread we didn't have money for soap. She said that once we got the typhus we wouldn't need money for soap and he said that once we got the typhus he'd never have to hear her complain again. My older brother told them that he didn't think married couples should argue the way they did.

Sometimes if the fight was bad my mother would lie down next to me and weep. I'd put my hand on her head and tell myself I didn't care what they did because I was going wherever I wanted and doing what I wanted.

But I wasn't sleeping because of the lice. My mother finally boiled my sweater, which was so infested we could see it moving, but the nits survived boiling and could only be ironed out. They made gray oily stains when they melted under the iron, and were only gone for a while, since whatever we disinfected just got reinfested by everything else. It was so bad around my waistband that I looked like I was always adjusting my pants. I woke up scratching. In the morning I ran my fingernails through my scalp and dropped what I pulled out onto the hot lid of the stove so I could see them sizzle.

I got on the tram still scratching and a Polish policeman told me to give him my coat. It was far too small to fit him and I showed him the elbows, which were worn through, and he said, 'Give it here anyway.' I said sure and added that I'd just come from the hospital and had the typhus. I combed my hair with my hand and wiped the lice on my sleeve and stepped closer to him and he moved to the rear of the car and got off at the next stop.

My father came home from the fabric factory with what he said was good news. His cousin had converted part of the factory floor into a dormitory for refugees who could pay and so he'd had to let some workers go but my father hadn't been one of them. He'd been worried about it because he and his cousin hadn't been getting along. To celebrate he brought home bread and onions and marmalade, which we hadn't seen since the rationing began, and which my brothers finished before I got back. We had the rest of the bread and onions with some kishke my mother made with steer intestines and some seasonings. My father didn't read from the newspaper. A German truck went by with a loudspeaker and its only message in Polish was that it was now forbidden to speak of 'the Jewish ghetto,' and the proper term was now 'the Jewish quarter.' 'How do you like it here in the Jewish quarter?' my father asked my mother. 'I find it confining,' she told him.

★ ★ ★

Lutek had arranged a way out of the ghetto even before it was sealed up. He showed me one morning in a downpour that had driven everyone else inside. Down an alley near Przejazd Street an apartment owner had built a cooplike shed with chicken wire and wood against the wall to keep people from stealing his rubbish bins, and inside the shed and behind the bins Lutek had chiseled out a passage that had started as a sewage drain. The smell was suffocating and when I first saw it I thought I'd never fit through. I had to go onto my back and push with my heels and squeeze one shoulder through at a time. I asked why he hadn't made it any bigger and he said it was a lot of work and that the smaller the better and easier to hide and he liked that only we could fit through. The shed had a roof, so once we were inside no one could see us. And he'd nailed a piece of tin over the gap so even someone inside wouldn't necessarily see it. I asked when he'd done this and he said after curfew. I said that it was amazing and he said yes, it was. I said he'd done all the work, and he agreed and said in honor of that our split would be seventy-thirty.

So for a few weeks we made out. He made a deal with some Polish boys, a gang from Łucka Street, and for five złotys a load they kept the blackmailers away. His father's friends brought us what they wanted to barter on the other side, and we took out linens and silverware and tools and pots and pans and whatever would fit through, and brought back flour and potatoes and milk and butter and onions and meat. Lutek could drag in twenty kilos of potatoes or onions in one go. Sometimes on the other side there were kids we recognized haggling and filling their sacks. Smaller kids hopped onto the wall and waited there like squirrels. When the police showed up everyone disappeared into their holes.

Other gangs heard about it and started using it. When we tried to stop them they beat us. When we came back with metal pipes they outnumbered us and were bigger besides. Once they'd taken it over they made such a racket going through that one kid got caught by the Jewish police and was turned over to a German who shot him in the face. We saw him later, still in the street, with his cheek open and his back on a sewer grate. I didn't want to look but Lutek stood over him with his hands on his hips like killing him had been his idea. Our hole had been sealed up with cement, and Lutek told me, 'Three weeks, every night I worked on that.'

First we were discouraged and then he said we'd been doing it the hard way and that one of his father's friends was now in the Jewish police and working the gate at Leszno Street. We watched him for a day or two. All three police forces had their sentry posts, German and Polish on one side and Jewish on the other. We called the Jews the yellow police because of their armbands and the Poles and Germans the blue and green police because of their uniforms. Lutek said the Jews were watched by the yellow police and the yellow police by the blue police and the blue police by the green police and the green police by the Gestapo. And where was the Gestapo? I wanted to know, and he said 'Aha!' as though I'd said something very smart. Everyone was always calling on everyone else to come over and translate for soldiers or work details passing through the gates, and during one shift the green and blue police had set up a business with Lutek's father's friend. 'So it's just a matter of everyone getting their taste,' Lutek said. Yellow took five, blue took ten, and green took twenty złotys per parcel. A good time to go through was when the guards had to search a lot of autos that were backed up. We just had to stand where we could see everything and then learn to wait, wait, wait. When it was safe to deal the friend would gesture for the blue policeman to come inside the gate and off we could go.

Lutek's father also told him about a new system for dealing with the blackmailers: once they surrounded us on the other side of the wall we called over the blue police and told them we were being robbed and that we wanted everyone taken to the station to sort things out. That was the code for the blue police to arrest us, and the blackmailers ran away. At the station we gave the blue police their cut and they let us go when the coast was clear.

We were waiting to go through a week later when Zofia and another girl with dark curly hair walked by with two baskets of goods. They set their baskets down, chatting and laughing, and the other girl shook out her hair like she'd just taken off a hat, and they pulled off their armbands and hoisted their loads again and walked right past all three sentry posts and out of the ghetto. The green policeman even said some kind of hello as they went by. Zofia waved and said something in response that he seemed to like.

The next day we visited her apartment to ask if she and her friend wanted to join our group. 'What group?' Zofia asked, and seemed unimpressed when I told her what we had going.

The new girl's name was Adina. She was from Baranowicze and you could tell she was from the east from her singsong way of speaking. She said she was a year older than us. She was pale and thin with sad black eyes. She didn't like to talk and always got angry when asked a question. She said that one day she'd come home late from dropping off some sewing and the Germans had driven her cousins out of town in a truck and forced them to jump into an open fire. Those who wouldn't jump were shot. A cousin who escaped into the woods had told her about it. Then her whole family had been herded west with other families through three villages and those who couldn't keep up were shot at like ducks until finally they were all loaded onto some trucks and driven into Warsaw. She said she'd brought her best clothes but that her mother had managed to bring only her

58

ceramic stew pot loaded with three bottles of cooking oil.

Lutek kept asking her about the fire part of her story until Zofia finally told him that if he didn't stop she'd throw him into a fire herself.

So I asked about the oil instead. 'What are you looking at?' Adina said to me, and made a face. 'He's in love,' Lutek told her. 'He worries me,' she told him back. 'Why would your mother save oil?' I asked her again.

She said her parents used to have a shop that sold oil her father had produced himself and was very proud of. He died before the war and the shop had gone downhill even before the Germans came. Her mother was bitter about it still and whenever anyone asked for credit or a favor, she always said, 'Sure, it's nice to screw on somebody *else's* sheets.' Lutek said that that could be our group motto and Zofia said again what made him think there was going to be a group.

'We might as well do something,' Adina told her. Back home she said that there'd always been something she needed to be doing but that here she went out into the street and then in no time at all she'd go back to their apartment again, since what was there for her to do in the street?

Lutek asked what made them think they

could just walk through the gates and Adina told him she'd always had a talent for that sort of thing. When they got to the city and passed through the center for refugees she told her mother that she'd hide their money and made sure she went first when her family had lined up to be searched, and a Volksdeutsche woman felt around in Adina's hair for a long time, as though she kept her treasures there, then found a bundle in the pocket of her skirt and pulled it free and exclaimed, 'And what are these? Diamonds?' and spilled them out onto a table only to discover they were hard candies. The other Volksdeutsche laughed and the woman slapped Adina's face and threw her out of the room without finding the gold coins she was also carrying.

* * *

We all worked together for a week and then an old Polish woman grabbed Adina and shouted, 'Smuggler! Smuggler!' when they were coming back through the gate, so Lutek grabbed the old woman and started shouting the same thing, and his father's friend had to drag all three over to the green and blue police to work the whole thing out. Zofia and I went a block away before stopping to watch.

The rule with us was always if one got stopped the others walked on. The old woman made a racket we could hear from there. Zofia said Lutek had dropped whatever he'd been carrying into her bag.

'This is going to take a while,' she said and I told her she was probably right. Neither of us had anywhere to go. She worried that Adina would be beaten even if they set her free and said she should've gone in her place. When she'd been caught, because of her looks the blue policeman had beaten her but not as a Jew.

'What makes old people like that?' she wondered. I told her I didn't know.

She said that a few days after the city surrendered, someone had told her mother that her father's father, her other grandfather, wanted to see her. Zofia had never met him. He was a rabbinical scholar, she never knew what sort.

I waited for her to go on. I was happy that we were talking like this.

She said her parents told her that this grandfather had a lot of money, she didn't know why, and that her mother was excited because maybe this would allow them all to emigrate. Zofia had never met him because when her father married someone non-Orthodox, his father told him that as far as he was concerned, his son had died, he'd already buried him and mourned his passing.

'So what was he like?' I asked.

'The one thing my father told me was that he wrote letters to God,' she said. 'That seemed like an interesting idea. I wondered what he did with them.'

'So what was he like?' I said.

'All my mother ever said about him was that he could dig money out of the ground,' she said. Some tram brakes screeched around the bend on Chłodna and when she touched her fingers to her mouth it made me wish she was somewhere quiet and safe. 'So now I was being summoned to see him, alone, and my mother was very excited and anxious and my father was angry with her for getting everyone stirred up. I remember them fussing about what I would wear and then I was delivered to a big dark house and told to go inside. An old woman opened the door and disappeared and I went up flights of stairs. I didn't know where I was going and I had to feel my way around the landings but I could see a light on the top floor. The top floor was a long dark room with angled ceilings. At the end of it an old man with a beard sat behind a desk piled with books. Some of the stacks reached the ceiling. There were stacks on the windowsills in the dormers. There were spiderwebs everywhere, even on his lamp, so I stopped to wait for him to say something. I finally said hello but for all I knew he was deaf. He looked up and gestured for me to come closer. I ducked under the webs as I went. When I was halfway there he held up his palm and I stopped and he watched me for a while. A clock was ticking somewhere in the room. I said hello to him again, then took a step, and again he held up his palm. So I told him who I was. His face didn't change and he waved his hand upward for me to go away. I took a step back, to see if that was really what he meant, and he went back to his reading.'

'So after all that he didn't even talk to you?' I said.

The green and blue police lost patience and started beating Adina and Lutek on their heads. Adina put her hands over her head, so one of them beat her hands. Then he stopped and everyone went back to their posts.

'I shouldn't even be with you, you're so unsanitary,' Zofia said to me. I put a hand to my neck, as if I could hide the lice.

Lutek and Adina disappeared down Żelazna Street and the old woman stood there talking to herself for a few more minutes before she finally left. Once she was gone, Zofia stood up and brushed the dirt from her skirt.

'When the war started, when it came to

food I was always more sly and would push through somehow, while my father and brother would stand and stand in the lines and get nothing,' she said. 'My mother thinks that what keeps me going is a well of spitefulness.' She thumped her chest. 'I think she's right. I can feel it right here.'

★ ★ ★

The typhus was everywhere worse and Zofia's building was filled with it. She carried around a tin of oil and paraffin to rub on herself to keep the lice away, and wouldn't let me sit anywhere nearby. She wouldn't let Lutek, either, but when she told him that he said, 'Who wants to?' We watched the street trading on Gęsia. In front of us a woman was selling children's underwear and the lining from a coat. When she saw us looking, she held up what she had as though it were a pot of gold and told us she must've gone out of her mind because she was giving these items away for almost nothing. A beggar beside her sat on his hands and held his cup with his bare feet. We were waiting there because someone was bringing us orders to fill and he was late.

'Maybe he's got the typhus too,' Zofia said, and Lutek said that the typhus was now the other subject he was sick of. Were we supposed to talk about nothing but food all day like him, Zofia wanted to know, and he said that he couldn't decide who was more boring. All the rich talked about was when they were going to get the inoculation and all the poor talked about was when they were going to get the disease.

My mother asked if my friends were clean and I told her *I* had more lice than anyone. So she dragged me back to the sink and doused my head and neck and chest again with kerosene. My brothers, about to leave for work, held me down and cheered her on.

'You *sound* good,' she said, once I got free and she listened to my breathing. She told me to stay away from the quarantined streets.

Zofia said that their house sanitary warden told her father that Krochmalna Street was the main incubator in the ghetto and that the Germans had said they'd burn it down if they could.

'I'm glad no one we know lives on Krochmalna Street,' I told her.

Adina said it was fenced off now, anyway, and they were taking everyone in big trucks to the baths on Spokojna. You could see she felt sorry for Zofia, who whenever she found a louse acted like it was the end of the world.

'Do the baths work?' Zofia asked.

Adina said that she'd asked someone that, but instead of answering he'd told her children and fish shouldn't have voices.

'The baths are where you catch the lice,' Lutek said. 'Or the delousing queues. And the sulphur they use doesn't kill anything anyway.'

'Shaved like a goy,' the beggar next to the woman sneered at him. 'Where are your peyes? Your family doesn't wear any? Maybe they're not the fashion anymore.'

'And what're you, the Rabbi of Warsaw? Shut your mouth,' Lutek told him.

The man we were waiting for never showed up and it came time for the new business we called Catching the Tram. We'd worked a deal with the blue policeman who escorted the number 10. Zofia had been the one to approach him. It was forbidden for Aryan trams to stop in the ghetto, but the 10 had to slow down to make the turn onto Zamen-hofa, where Adina kept watch and left her hat on if all was clear, and then Lutek and I ran out for the sacks thrown off.

We got caught one day by the green police and they chased Lutek instead of me and I hid in a shop that sold matches and cigarettes and small bottles of homemade medicine until the owner thought I was waiting to steal something and threw me out. A yellow policeman who'd been standing next to his bicycle with a young woman walked over to me. He was wearing his own jacket and trousers with the yellow uniform cap and armband. He was shorter than I was and had huge ears. He took my sleeve and asked what I had in the sack and I told him I had to leave. He smiled and held up a finger, showing off for the woman. She wasn't very tall but she was taller than he was.

'You don't recognize me?' he said, and then I did: he'd been one of the foremen at my father's cousin's factory, the one who'd sent me to the cloth-scraping. His name was Lejkin.

'I like your boots,' I told him.

'So does she,' he said, and the woman blushed. 'You know what they say: a constable in shoes is only a half constable.'

I told him again that I had to go. He said I didn't, in fact, and that I could either get on the handlebars and come with him or walk with him over to the next block, where he would tell the Germans he'd found a smuggler.

Come with him where, I asked, and he said he'd give me a ride home. I asked him why and he said that he liked doing favors for people. 'We short fellows have to stick together,' he said. He strapped my sack of onions to a rack over his back wheel and tipped his cap to the woman. Then he steadied the handlebars so I could sit on them. I wanted to tell him his bicycle was too big for him but I was afraid he would turn me over to the Germans.

'See you soon,' he said to the woman and she laughed and said, 'We'll see,' as he started pedaling away.

I was so bony the handlebars hurt on the cobblestones. I couldn't tell if any of my friends had seen what had happened.

He asked if I knew anyone else in the Jewish Order Service. I told him no. He asked if a lot of young men I knew wanted to be in the Order Service. I told him no. He pedaled for a while and then said that it was odd: he'd only got the job because his cousin had entered his name on a list. Someone had handed him a hat and a yellow armband and a rule book and just like that he was on duty.

'Of course we had some training,' he added when I didn't say anything.

'You're going to find me a bootjack,' he said a few blocks later, after he dropped me in front of my building. 'I need a proper bootjack.'

'How would I know where to find a bootjack?' I asked him.

'How does one know where to find anything?' he answered. 'Look around. Say hello to your father for me.' Then he flicked my nose with his finger, pushed himself off, and rode away.

★ ★ ★

Given the news that apartments were going to be requisitioned anyway, my father said he'd gone looking for boarders who could pay a little something, that it'd be nice if a Jew saw a herring on his table even once a week. My mother said she would only agree to it if whoever he found first went through the disinfection units and then presented her with their debusing certificates. She thought this would be the end of that problem, since the lines at those stations made you wait all day and night, but a family of four showed up the next morning and handed her their certificates one by one as they passed into our apartment carrying what they had. They were each wearing many layers, both for the cold and to make it easier to carry other things. They didn't look clean, but as my father told her, they weren't any dirtier than anyone else, either. 'They probably bought their certificates, instead of waiting in line,' my mother said, which was what my father and I assumed, though we only shrugged.

They brought as an offering overcooked

kasha with rutabaga preserves, some stuffed cabbage that was much more appetizing, and a tiny jar of honey that the father said we might want to use as barter.

He was a tall man who made jokes and his wife was short and had angry eyes and looked disappointed by everything in our apartment. She looked at our kitchen and said, 'Ice in the pot, frozen taps, and not a drop of water.' Their daughter said she was nineteen and their son said he was hungry. He was about my age. Once he was eating he told us his name was Boris.

His parents and sister took the kitchen and my mother and father were in the bedroom so the rest of us slept in the hall, It was even colder there. His feet were in my face. In the middle of the night he seemed to know that I was still awake and started talking in a low voice. He said his family had taken over the previous apartment they'd been in, that they'd just stormed the place with another family. Then it had been taken away from them by the Germans. He said in the shelter at the synagogue all of the boys stole bread from one another's families, and what they didn't eat they traded for horseshoe spikes they used in games. He said he'd got the honey outside the ghetto when an O.D. man had turned his back and pretended not to see him coming or going. I asked what an O.D. man was and it turned out that's what he called the yellow police, because of the German name for them, Ordnungsdienst, the Order Service. After we listened to my brothers snore he asked if I thought he looked strong.

'Are you talking to me?' I asked. He said he was. He asked again if I thought he looked strong. I told him I guessed so.

He said that that was because he was. 'Smugglers eat more than other people because they work harder,' he said. His cheeks had the pockmarks from chicken pox and he had an expression like he was sharing the floor with a sick person.

I told him smugglers didn't usually tell everyone that they were smugglers, and he snorted. 'I don't think you're Gestapo,' he said.

'You never know,' I told him.

He asked how long we'd lived there. He said he'd hated his village and that when he and his friends trampled their neighbor's vegetable garden the neighbor had come out of his house and tried to beat them with a leather strap. Then he turned loose his dog, who bit them. Dogs hate the poor, he added, thinking about it further. He talked with his hands, like a Jew.

He said he'd been thrown out of the Polish

Scouting Association after being told that as a Jew he couldn't be sworn in on a Christian bible and he suggested to his troop leader that they use a spare-parts catalog instead. He said his only real friend hadn't shown up to say goodbye on the day he left. He said all of this gave him an advantage because he never felt homesick. And it was better to have no one to miss.

He said his father had a weakness for the bottle and I'd probably already noticed that he never refused a toast. 'And why should he?' he asked.

If he was waiting for an argument, he didn't get one from me. 'You're soon going to have trouble with my mother, too,' he told me. He said it was never long before she was sure she was being cheated and that's why she was always shouting at someone. I asked if we were going to have trouble with his sister, too, and he said she was so shy she'd told him that if she ever got married she wanted it to be in a cellar where no one would see.

I asked what happened to his sister's hand and he said that on the way to Warsaw his father had let him take the reins of the wagon and that he had steered the thing so badly when crossing a bridge that he'd turned them over into a ditch.

I asked how they'd managed to get the

wagon back on its wheels and he said he told people stories like that because he thought it was important to be clear in your own head on what you could and couldn't do and this was how he'd grown up to be someone with open eyes. Inasmuch as he'd grown up at all, I said, and he told me he'd show me how much he'd grown up the next chance he got.

I told our group about him and repeated some of his stories and Lutek said I should bring him along tomorrow. Adina wanted to know why and he said she shouldn't worry about it, since Sh'maya's friend Boris probably wasn't going to survive long anyway, given what we were up to.

'Why're you calling me that?' I asked.

'Isn't that what your brothers call you?' he said.

When everyone was asleep that night, I told Boris he should come meet the group. He said he looked forward to becoming our leader. I told him that as far as he was concerned school was starting once the sun came up the next morning, so he should get some rest.

★ ★ ★

My mother and father were upset by the news that the three tramlines for the Jews were going to be shut down, and in the worst part of the winter. My mother asked why she had to live to see such awful years and my father told her there were probably worse years to come. The tramlines were to be replaced with just one that was given no number but only a shield with the Star of David. Lutek said our bigger worry was that they would stop running the Aryan trams through the ghetto, and a month later they did.

There was no announcement, so we waited for three days before figuring that out for ourselves. Then Zofia asked what we would do now and Boris said we could start by not playing so nice. To show us what he meant he went along when Lutek delivered our last sack from off the tram and told the men who'd ordered it that they couldn't have it until we got more money.

'We agreed to what we agreed to,' one of them told him.

'*They* agreed to it. *I* didn't agree to it,' he said, and Lutek told us they went back and forth about it and the men made some threats but eventually got scared by all the patrols coming and going. He said Boris held everyone up like he didn't even notice the police until he got what he wanted; not only an extra bag of potatoes but also some raisin wine. He shared both with the rest of us.

At dinner my father told us it seemed like no matter where he went, German soldiers followed. My mother got alarmed and asked why and he said he had no idea.

Boris's family was in the back room talking in low voices, and my father said, 'Maybe they're planning a coup.'

My mother again brought up the idea of getting Aryan papers and told us Czerniaków's sister-in-law had assured her it could be done and for not much money, but when she said how much it was, my father asked, 'For each person?' so loud that she had to shush him. She told him that was what a birth certificate and an identity card cost. She said there were cheaper ones but they looked suspicious even at a glance.

My father asked how she thought we would eat while we saved that much money and who we would contact on the other side to help us, or would we be all alone. He pointed at me and said, 'And do you think this one can pass?' He reminded her she'd said about me that the minute I opened my mouth you could hear the Jew in me.

My mother looked at me sadly and said, 'Aron, what do you think?'

'I think we're doing all right here,' I told

her. I could feel my ears burning.

'There,' my father said. 'Even he thinks we should stay.'

My mother said she would ask my brothers when they got home but I could tell by her voice that she'd already given up.

But they never got home because they were picked up on the street outside our apartment by soldiers and the yellow police for the work battalions. We heard the shouting but didn't understand what it was. My mother pulled me from the window and then our neighbor rushed in to tell us. She said that another man had pulled money from his pocket and handed some to each of the soldiers and policemen and they'd let him go.

She thought they were taking them to Józefów. At least that was what one of the police had told her. My father pulled all the money we had from our hiding places and rushed off to try to catch them before they got to the police station. I ran after him. It was almost curfew.

The column was being marched double-time and the yellow police were in the back, shouting and thumping with fat sticks the ones who didn't keep up. The Germans at the front every so often looked back and then there was more shouting and thumping.

'Listen,' my father called when he got close

enough to the last yellow policeman.

'Go away or you'll end up with them,' the man warned him. My father lagged back but I took the money from his hand and passed him because I'd noticed Lejkin up ahead.

'Look who it is,' Lejkin said when I fell into step alongside him. 'Do you want to go to a labor camp? Where's my bootjack?'

'I found a beautiful one,' I told him. 'But I also have a deal for you.' I showed him the money I held inside my coat.

'Who's being saved?' he asked. I pointed out my brothers a few rows up. In their misery they still hadn't seen us. 'And what's in it for me?' he added.

'More where this came from,' I told him. Though as far as I knew we didn't have any more.

He let us march another street just to let me suffer and then said something to the trailing policeman and they both went forward and pulled my brothers from the line and dragged them back to my father, who made such a cry of happiness and relief that he almost gave the whole thing away.

★   ★   ★

'I need a bootjack,' I told Lutek.

'A bootjack?' he said. 'What do you need

77

with a bootjack?' We were standing next to each other to get warm back at our old Leszno Street gate. It was snowing, Lutek was trying to get our old arrangement going again, but his father's friend had more business than he knew what to do with so he was making us wait. Lutek kept bringing up phlegm and spitting it onto the pavement to watch it freeze. Our shoes were soaked through and coming apart and we were stamping our feet.

'I have a contact that maybe we can use,' I told him.

'Who would that be?' he asked.

'Someone I met. You don't have to know everything,' I told him.

'Going into business for yourself?' he said.

'You don't tell me about everyone you meet,' I said. I didn't know why I wasn't telling him.

'That's true,' he said.

'So are you going to help me or not?' I asked.

He blew on his hands and rubbed his cheeks and then gave me the address of a shop on Niska. 'Bring something to trade,' he told me. Then something caught his eye across the square. 'He's ready for us,' he said.

★ ★ ★

My parents had been so happy at my brothers' return that they celebrated even with Boris's family. My father suggested we open the honey, but Boris's father said that we should save it for a bigger occasion. Like maybe the end of the war, my brother said, then added that he'd heard there'd been a recent bombardment of Berlin. He was always talking about new peace proposals he'd heard had been offered through the Swedes or the Swiss or the pope. Everyone sat around the table smoking their cigarettes and telling everyone else what they'd heard. My father always said that if you gave Jews a minute to themselves they produced rumors, Boris's mother said the rabbi in their village had predicted a year earlier that the war would end this month because his cabalistic calculations had proved the cup of Jewish suffering was now entirely full. Her husband cheered ironically and proposed a toast to the news. He poured a little bit of vodka for himself and my father.

When their toast was drunk he said, 'So Hitler asks the governor-general what's being done to oppress the Jews. The governor-general talks about all the rights and privileges that have been taken away but Hitler's unsatisfied. The governor-general talks about everything that's been stolen from the Jews and Hitler's still unsatisfied. He talks about the ghetto and all the disease and filth and Hitler's still unsatisfied. Finally the governor-general says, 'Oh, and I've also set up a Jewish Self-Aid Organization,' and Hitler exclaims, 'Now you've got it!''

My brothers laughed with him. 'Here's to the Jewish police as well,' my father said grimly when they stopped.

We were all quiet. Outside we could hear the street vendor calling out his coke and carbide for sale. 'Well, that helped the party along,' Boris's father said.

My mother had recovered enough by then to smile. 'At first I liked the idea of Jewish police,' she finally said. 'If you have to take orders from a Pole or a Jew, why not a Jew? And they didn't turn over the merchants' baskets and trample everyone's goods.'

'That was before they started rounding up everyone too poor to buy themselves out of a trip to the labor camps,' my father said.

'Yes, that was before,' my mother said. And then the party really was over. Later she asked my father again if he could get me back into the factory and when he said he was lucky to still have a position there she lost her temper and asked what he was going to do on the day when I didn't come home. He told her they weren't rounding up children for the labor camps and reminded her that at my size I looked even younger than I was.

'If something happens to him I will never look at you again,' my mother said.

'You never look at me now,' my father said.

'We're trying to sleep out here,' one of my brothers called from where we were lying in the hallway.

'They fight like my parents,' Boris said, and in the dark it sounded like he was waiting for me to agree.

'I think he's asleep,' my brother finally said.

'He's not asleep,' Boris told him.

★ ★ ★

Because my mother was so unhappy I introduced her to Zofia and Adina, both of whom she liked more than Lutek, as I knew she would. Adina said, 'Why are we meeting your mother? Are we getting engaged?' but Zofia said she understood and told Adina that doing something nice for someone wouldn't kill her. We met in a café and my mother insisted on buying the girls tea even though I could see how upset she was at what she spent. She asked after their families and made her *such a shame* face when she heard their sad stories. Then when our visit was almost over she said that her friend who was Czerniaków's sister-in-law had told her about the performances at Janusz Korczak's orphanage and would we all like to go?

Adina looked at me and my expression told her I'd had no idea that my mother was going to do this.

'I don't think the girls want to see children's puppet shows,' I said to my mother.

'They're not *puppet* shows,' she said.

'I saw their parade when they had to move into the ghetto,' Zofia told her. 'It was quite the circus.'

'I saw that too,' I said. 'Did you see the wagons with the geraniums?'

Zofia said that she'd heard all sorts of rumors about him: he'd been taken into the forest and shot; he'd been taken away to one of the camps; he'd been put on a boat to Palestine. The problem had been that he'd gone all the way to the Gestapo to protest the confiscation of some potatoes and showed up there having refused to wear his armband. It turned out that he'd been beaten and thrown into a cell but then after a month they'd let him go.

'They let him go?' Adina asked, interested in that part. 'Why?'

Zofia held her hand up and rubbed her thumb against her fingertips.

'Is he rich?' Adina asked.

'He has rich friends,' Zofia told her. She said she'd also heard that his Polish caretaker had been beaten almost to death on the same day because he'd applied in person to go into the ghetto with the rest of the orphanage but Aryans could no longer work for Jews.

The four of us listened to the conversations at other tables. I could see my mother's disappointment in her eyes. 'Working and stealing, working and stealing, that's what times are like now,' she said. The girls just looked at her and finished their tea. Zofia kept the sugar cube pressed between her lips and her tongue poked out only once it had completely dissolved. My mother stood up and wiped her eyes. Well, she told us, if we were interested, the new orphanage was now on Chłodna Street, in the small ghetto.

'We'll go,' Zofia said. 'Sure. It could be fun.' Adina looked at her. 'It could be fun,' Zofia repeated.

My mother was pleased and left before we could change our minds. Adina said, 'You're not going to get Lutek and Boris to agree,' and Zofia said, 'I'm not going to try.'

That night at dinner my mother told everyone the good news and Boris's father wanted to know why the Germans would let Korczak go.

'Maybe they made him an informer,' Boris said.

'Maybe he gave them a pile of gold,' my brother said.

'The Germans know him as the greatest child specialist and educational reformer in all of Europe,' my father said. 'They know him even in England and France. He's probably the safest Jew in the ghetto.'

'A big shot,' Boris said.

'Was he the one with the scandal before the war?' Boris's father asked.

'What scandal?' my mother asked. Boris's father held up his hands like he meant no offense.

'He lost his radio program and his position on the juvenile court,' my father said. 'He went on a trip to Palestine and then people no longer overlooked that Janusz Korczak the Pole was really Henryk Goldszmit the Jew.'

Shots were fired outside and we all were quiet around the table, listening. The soup was beet shavings and nettle leaves with little lumps of kasha.

'No one wanted a Jew in charge of Poland's juvenile offenders,' my father added. But I was still thinking about why the Germans would let Korczak go and everyone else had gone on to thinking about other things.

* ★ ★

At the orphanage a line had been painted through the sign for the Roesler Commercial Secondary School and a handmade wooden sign that said *The Children's Republic* hung below it from twine. We were escorted into the building and to wooden folding chairs in front of the stage by little girls in costumes made of bits of paper and other scraps. 'What are you supposed to be?' I asked the girl leading me in. Her paper was mostly colored green and she said, 'I'm a dragon.'

The stage was a platform at the end of the main room on the first floor. Once all of the chairs were filled and people lined the back wall, the heavy woman I'd seen the Old Doctor pulling down the street came through a door in the back and everyone applauded. She was carrying a cactus that she set down on the front of the stage. She welcomed everyone to the Orphans' Home and said her name was Stefania Wilczyńska and that she was the senior teacher. She introduced the cactus as her favorite orphan and the home's good-luck charm, and everyone laughed as though they knew what she was talking about. Then she said it was her pleasure to introduce the greatest humanist and intellectual in Poland.

Everyone applauded again and Korczak came through the same door. He was wearing a paper crown, and people laughed at that. The heavy woman took a seat in the front row.

'Someone should give that fat man in the back a chair,' Korczak said. 'He looks much too well-to-do to stand.' The smaller children in the audience thought he was hilarious.

'Everyone loves my rude remarks,' he said once they quieted down. 'Even the dressed-up ladies and elegant gentlemen. Though they keep their distance and I never hear from them until their children are sick. Then it's, 'Please, please, you have to come,' even if it's the middle of the night.'

'So he's a doctor?' Adina whispered to my mother.

My mother told her he was a famous doctor and he'd been an army doctor in the war between Russia and Japan and in the world war, and in the civil war in Russia.

He apologized to what he called the better society in the crowd for his occasional use of Yiddish. He said he would like to present one of his radio talks, called *The Loneliness of the Child*, before standing aside for the main event of the evening, the home's production that would showcase the most talented undersized citizens who had been gathered from Warsaw's attics and basements. 'That's where you find some of the city's most interesting people,' he said. 'Forgotten, in someone's basement.' He cleared his throat and cleaned his glasses with a handkerchief, taking his time. Then he put his glasses back on and began.

It was funny at first but then got sadder, I stopped listening.

When it was over everyone applauded again and the children set up the stage for the play.

'I liked when he said that loneliness was the port from which he always sets out,' Zofia said.

'I liked when he asked, 'Do you steer the course or are you just carried along?'' my mother said.

'I'm not just carried along,' Adina said.

'You sound like Boris,' Zofia said.

The play was called *The Three Journeys of Hershkele*. The hero, who wore a headdress he could barely keep on his head and that was never explained, hid on a plane bound for England, where he talked the English king into allowing all the Jews to emigrate to Palestine. Then he hid on a plane to Egypt, where he found a whole roomful of the pharoah's gold to pay for everyone's trip. Then he hid on a plane to Germany, where he met with Hitler. The boy who played Hitler was very good. When he saw all the gold Hitler was sorry for what he'd done and invited the Jews back, and the hero told him no thanks but said he'd use the leftover gold to buy milk and butter for the starving German children. At the end just the hero and Hitler remained onstage and Hitler thanked him and asked if there was anything he could do in return for the milk and butter and the hero said yes, that Hitler could make a law that all adults who pass children on the street must bend their heads in shame, and Hitler said that he would. Then the hero sang a song about the Ten Commandments and the whole cast did a dance and the thing was over.

My mother applauded even after everyone else had stopped. She was weeping again. 'You liked it too,' she said to me. Korczak came back out to thank the cast of the play and everyone applauded again. He thanked everyone for coming, and congratulated them all on being twice orphaned themselves, since they were stateless and Jewish. He told the adults to remember to approach children with affection for what they already were and with respect for what they could become. He told the children to remember that we couldn't leave the world the way we found it.

And to remember to wash our hands. And to drink boiled water. And to open the windows to get fresh air. He looked out the window closest to him and finished by saying that we should wait until it was warmer, though.

★　★　★

Even Adina thought the old doctor had been worthwhile, even if part of the reason for that had been the cookies afterwards. Later she said she hadn't seen cookies in she didn't know how long and Boris got angry that we hadn't swiped some for him and Lutek. When Zofia told him they weren't really cookies, Adina said maybe they weren't cookies but they'd been close enough.

We were all hungry all the time. 'I remember Mama fed us vegetables because she thought they were healthy,' Adina told us one morning, like she'd had a dream. We were in front of a shop for hernia belts and someone was shouting at their kids from the building's roof. Someone behind us on the first floor kept telling his wife to add water to the carbide lamp. Someone else poured dirty oil from a windowsill higher up and it spattered on the pavement near our feet.

Boris got us started trading the ration cards of people who'd died or left the ghetto, and

89

he thought the best place was around the distribution shops when the mothers came by with their small children, and he was right. He and Lutek did the haggling because the rest of us couldn't stand to see the kids' faces while it went on. Lutek had got one boy's wooden shoes by holding the ration cards under his mother's nose and saying he was only asking her to throw in one extra item, and that if she wanted to trade she had to be able to imagine herself in another guy's shoes. She'd taken the cards and used them for rutabagas and her son had gone home barefoot. But it was getting warmer, Zofia said it was already late in May though Boris thought it was still April. Lutek tried on the wooden shoes and said that just as he thought, they fitted perfectly.

'What is *he* contributing?' Boris said to Lutek, meaning me. But the girls told him to leave me alone.

'My sister hated spinach,' Adina said. 'But I liked it.'

'Are you still talking about that?' Boris wanted to know.

'My mother used to tell me I had to be so clean that my knees would shine,' Zofia said.

I could see the lice where her hair was parted. 'You're still pretty clean,' I told her.

Lutek told us their apartment was now

cleaner because his father and some of the other porters had taken to using sawdust ovens, which were also cheaper than coal.

'Do those keep you warm?' Adina asked.

'Nothing keeps you warm,' he told her.

'The ovens aren't the problem,' Boris said. 'Hello, Mother,' he said to a woman who came out of the shop with three small children, all of them weeping. 'Is there any way *I* can be of help?'

After they left he held up a heavy shawl. 'It's English,' he said, showing us the label. He and Lutek went back and forth over whether he might have given the mother less.

We said goodbye an hour before curfew and I was halfway home when someone grabbed my collar. 'I like my bootjack,' Lejkin said.

'I'm glad to hear it,' I told him, pulling free. 'I have to get home.'

'You always have to get home,' Lejkin said, as though this was some ongoing mystery.

He walked along beside me, eating something that he didn't offer to share.

'My friends on Krochmalna Street want to keep better track of who's doing what at the different gates,' he said. He meant the yellow police, who had moved their headquarters there in January. I knew because Lutek now took a different route through the small ghetto.

'What's that to me?' I asked.

'You seem to be all over the place,' he said. 'I just thought you might notice things.'

'I'm bad at noticing things,' I told him.

'Well, whatever you do notice,' he said.

I kept walking. I stopped at the tram stop, but no one was waiting there. I'd probably missed it.

'It's just a matter of keeping track of things,' he said. 'It's not as though anyone intends to do anything that's bad for business.'

I waited for a few minutes more and then started walking again. The top of one shoe had come completely loose and flapped with every step.

'There are also opportunities I could let you know about when they arise,' he said. 'There are some confiscated onions right now, for example, that haven't yet been turned in.'

'I think *you're* the one who's all over the place,' I told him.

He shrugged like he was used to those kinds of compliments. 'The Jewish Order Service, by the way, also has the responsibility of deciding which apartments to requisition, in terms of the further resettlement of the incoming population,' he said.

'Well, our apartment's already packed,' I said.

'Oh, some apartments are fifteen and twenty to a room,' he told me. 'You can't imagine.'

I stopped and tried to rewrap the cloth strips around my shoe. I couldn't believe I was crying about a shoe.

'And of course there's always the question of what your friends might do once they hear you're working with the Service,' he said. And when I didn't answer that either he said, 'Or have you already told them?

'Well, think about it,' he said a block or two later, when I still hadn't spoken. And when I looked back again after another half a block he was gone.

*   *   *

There was a commotion by my building, a group of Germans were kicking at something between them and screaming in German at whatever they were kicking. I hadn't heard men screaming like that before. People stopped on the street to watch. I didn't want to get too close but they were in front of my door.

It was someone on his side on the

cobblestones and when he made a noise like he was in pain I knew it was my father. I stopped and then pushed closer like someone in line for the tram. After a few more kicks the Germans stayed in a circle around him but talked with each other instead of screaming. While they inspected him he crawled around their legs. He saw me but didn't make any sign. The feeling that I should do something lifted me onto my toes. I wanted to but when the time came to do it I lost my nerve. I stood there in the middle of the street.

He had his knees up and his shoulders hunched and a German gave him one more kick that spun him around. Then he just lay there. I thought a son would go to him or scream at the Germans himself. They exchanged a few more comments with some curious Germans on the other side of the street. Then they all started shoving and haranguing one another and left.

A few people approached him, including me. The sleeves and back of his coat were soaked in mud. 'Don't,' he said when I reached to help him up. He got onto his hands and knees and then his feet, tipping around a little, and then headed off away from our door.

I followed him. His walk got more like his

old walk. At the first corner we came to, he turned and I caught up with him. Every so often I looked up at his face. He turned again at the next corner, and then again. When the fourth turn brought us back to our street, he stopped to make sure the Germans were gone. At our door he had me go up the front steps ahead of him.

My mother asked what had happened and he told her he'd been knocked down by a wagon. She got upset and boiled some water to help him clean himself up and said he could've been killed. He told her to sew some patches on my coat's elbows, and that everything was sticking out on me. He washed his face at the sink for a long time. My mother was also upset about his coat, which was not only muddy but also had lost one of its pockets. She moaned and carried on about the lining and finally my father shouted at her to stop going on and on about the *coat*, and she was scared and hurt enough that she didn't say anything else.

Boris's father poked his head in to ask if everything was okay. When no one answered, Boris called from the hallway, 'He got hit by a wagon.' My father went back to washing his face.

For a time afterwards whenever I closed my eyes I saw him on the street. I couldn't sleep at night, such strange thoughts kept coming into my head. I woke with blood in my mouth and my mother said it looked like I'd bitten my tongue.

He was different after that and didn't go back to work for a few days. He sat at the kitchen table by the window with his back to everyone holding a wet cloth to his head and nursing a cup of tea my mother made him. She said it was all right and that we just needed to give him some room. He looked at me sometimes as if the Germans had kicked the courage out of both of us. When Boris and I left the apartment and I said goodbye, he gave a little wave.

In June it got so hot no one could sleep, then on the one night it got cooler the Germans decided to move their whole army past our apartment.

All night tanks ground through the streets and over the Vistula bridge. Trucks thundered along behind them. We all went to the window to watch; you couldn't rest anyway. The whole apartment shook and anything that was loose jingled and rattled. We had to take our teacups down from the shelf. Every few hours my mother exclaimed about how long it was going on. At first my father tried to stay in bed but even he had to get up after a while. Once the sun came up all of us except my mother went down to the street to get a better view.

The procession went on until noon. All the Germans in Germany were being trucked through to somewhere. Boris's father said that never in his life had he seen such machines as the Germans had, but I could barely hear him because of the noise. Soldiers hung off everything everywhere. No one could cross the street. A stray dog tried it at a run and almost lost its tail.

All sorts of German slogans were painted in white on the tanks' sides. The one we saw most often was STALIN, WIR KOMMEN.

Some of the smaller kids got excited by the huge trucks that were pulling gigantic cannons. The diesel exhaust was dark brown and gave us all headaches, so we went back inside.

That night we heard explosions in the city and the next morning were told that the Russians had bombed Warsaw. Bombs had fallen on Okęcie, Teatralny Square, and a tram near the Kierbedź Bridge, killing everyone on board.

'Why do you keep going on about your mother?' Boris asked later that morning. 'Do you think we all want to hear about your mother? Don't we all have mothers to worry about?'

'I certainly have to worry about mine,' Adina agreed.

The streets were full of sick people and everyone said the typhus was still spreading. My father had told my mother that God drowned the mangy to save the rest of the flock and my mother had slapped him. I'd told the gang about it. 'And your father just let her slap him?' Boris asked. He thought even the typhus might bring us some business and again he turned out to be right when Lejkin came to my apartment and said the Service was recruiting a special unit that would hang disinfection and quarantine signs for extra ration cards. He let me bring along the whole group and we hung signs for three days. 'How did he come to find you?' Zofia wanted to know while we were hanging one over a disinfection station.

'Maybe he likes me,' Hold her.

'No one likes you,' Boris said.

'He makes a good point,' Adina said.

I used my extra cards to buy rye flour, kasha, and potatoes, Boris brought a plateful of meat soup home for each member of his family.

My mother checked us all for rashes. She rubbed my hand raw to recheck a spot she was anxious about. 'The Germans threw us all on top of one another and turned loose the epidemic they were trying to prevent,' she said.

'Won't they be shocked to hear that,' my father told her.

Zofia's mother brought Salcia to the hospital for a blood infection and was told that none of the hospitals had room any longer for other kinds of sick people. All four were now only epidemic hospitals. She said that her father was heartbroken because both of the Brysz girls had died in the Stawld hospital.

'Who are the Brysz girls?' I asked, and she reminded me. 'Now I remember,' I told her.

'Sh'maya thinks only of himself,' she said, and Boris and Lutek laughed.

'Aron,' I said. 'Aron thinks only of himself.'

'Don't you ever think about anyone else?' she asked. 'In you Moses dies of thirst and the tablets turn to sand.'

'What does that mean?' I wanted to know.

'It's something my grandfather used to say,' she said. 'When someone disappointed him.'

'What did I do?' I said.

'You disappointed her,' Boris explained.

'What does everyone understand that I don't?' I said. I was tired of being the one that no one cared about. Especially her. I wanted to hit someone.

'You keep acting as though everything is normal,' Zofia said.

'Why do you say that about me and not the others?' I asked.

'Oh, stop pestering me,' she said.

'I'm not pestering you,' I told her.

'And go wash yourself,' she said, then took Adina's hand and left.

★　★　★

Someone pounded on our door the next morning before it was fully light. My mother had to step over me in the hallway to see who it was. When she opened the door a German said to her, 'I need twenty people.' His Polish was lousy but we understood him. He looked at us on the floor and then stepped over us and searched the apartment. He switched to German in the bedrooms, saying 'Raus, raus.' He took my father and brothers and Boris's father out into the hall with him. Before they shut the door we could see a yellow policeman out there too. They talked and my mother went from the door to the stove to the door again and then my father came back in and said, 'They told us we're all going into a labor battalion for a few days and that everything's going to be all right. We're going to be working and we're going to be fed.'

'Oh no, oh no, oh no, oh no,' my mother said, and Boris shouted for someone to shut the door, that there was a draft.

'Stop,' my father told her. 'At least with the Germans we know we'll get a noontime meal. A little hot soup or something.' She argued with him but he told her the work detail was good news since those coming back could smuggle food with them. He kissed her and bent down and kissed me. He looked into my eyes like he was going to say something, then stood up and stepped out into the hallway and shut the door behind him.

Afterwards my mother looked at us like disaster was coming out of the walls. 'Get her out of here,' Boris's mother finally told me. 'I'll finish the cleaning. Go stand in line somewhere,' she told my mother, and pulled the rag from her hands. 'Do something to feed your family.'

My mother sat at the kitchen table with her palms over her face. 'Come on,' I told her. 'There's no point in waiting around with folded hands.'

This was one of her sayings and it got her to her feet. She found her hat and bag and led me out the door.

The shops on Gęsia were empty and the cartons on display in the windows were labeled EMPTY BOXES. A woman who was sweeping rubbish back and forth outside one of the shops with an old straw broom told her some meat was being brought in on Grzybowska from one of the slaughterhouses later that morning, so we walked all the way over there.

On Dzielna we passed a crowd around two women ladling out gray milk from a dirty can. My mother read their cardboard sign and then led me away, saying they were asking too much.

She talked to herself while she walked. She said that it didn't cost us a thing to look. She said maybe they'd put the horsemeat in vinegar and water so it would soften up.

She fixed her shoe in front of a photographic studio in an arcade. The window display said WEHRMACHT SOLDATEN. A rickshaw went by and she complained that everyone who had an arm and a leg had hopped up on a bicycle and made like a Chinese coolie.

'Your poor father,' she said.

'You're still limping,' I told her.

'They should only be taking single men. At first they were only taking single men for the work details,' she said. 'So there were a lot of weddings.'

'Do you need to fix your shoe again?' I said.

'How're yours?' she asked.

'The twine worked,' I told her.

We passed a boy violinist playing 'Ba'al Shem Tov' for coins. He stopped playing until I moved farther away from his cup.

'I don't know why the Germans always find your father,' she said. 'On the Sabbath two of them beat him for not saluting.'

'I saw the marks,' I said.

'Another beat him because he did salute,' she said. 'That one told him, 'You're not in my army.''

'Almost everyone comes back from the work details in two or three days,' I finally told her.

'I thought they'd stay here a few months, make us work hard and then leave and we'd have our peace back,' she said.

'The Germans?' I said. She didn't answer.

'Do you think your friend in the Jewish police could help us find out where they took them?' she asked. 'The little pisher with the big ears?'

'He's not my friend,' I said. 'How do you know about him?'

'He said he was,' she said. 'He came by looking for you.'

'What did he want?' I asked.

'I just said he wanted to find you,' she told me. 'Maybe this place,' she said, and stepped into an apartment building. But the shop that had been there was gone. Instead there was a small round table in a bare room with an old man who'd tried to hide his beard by wrapping a rag around his face like he had a toothache.

'Your friend's one of those smart policemen who don't like having to order people around and so are always telling you why something has to be done,' she said once we were back out on the street. 'You can see in their eyes that they want to show

104

it's not up to them.'

'He's not my friend,' I told her. 'But if I see him I'll ask if he knows anything.'

She led us onto the wooden bridge across Przebieg Street and stopped at the top next to other people who were looking out at the Vistula. We watched a barge float down the river. We could see a little green on the other side. She put a hand on my shoulder and I put one on her back.

Finally we came down off the bridge. 'When I was a girl and I was hungry I just stood in front of pastry shops,' she told me. 'As if just looking would fill me up. One time I ate pickles I stole from a barrel and got diarrhea.'

'I guess that taught you not to steal,' I said.

'Stealing is always wrong,' she said.

'Starving is always wrong,' I told her.

She asked if I knew they now said, 'He sold the pot from his kitchen,' instead of 'He sold the shirt off his back,' since without a pot you have nothing to cook with.

'I did know that,' I told her.

'It's hard to keep the peace at mealtimes if families have to look at other families' fuller plates,' she said.

I was sick of everything, including her. I walked with her like she was my biggest problem.

She looked at me like she knew what I was thinking. 'I'm angry at the rich for not doing their duty for the poor,' she finally said.

'Why should they help us?' I asked.

'You can hear the street children, hungry all night,' she said.

'Who isn't,' I said.

'The rich people,' she said. 'And they should help more than they do.'

On Grzybowska we didn't see anyone and then two men gestured us into an apartment where two women were already arguing with them around an open barrel.

'It's meat,' one of the men said. 'You grind it up and it's still meat.'

'You should be ashamed,' one of the women said. 'I'm not eating ground-up assholes.'

'No one said you had to eat anything,' the man told her.

My mother pulled me back out onto the street. 'There's another shop on Ceglana,' she said. Her face made me ashamed of how I'd been thinking. We took turns squeezing each other's hand as we walked. When we came to a long line I asked if this was it.

'This is the place,' she said.

Kids went up and down the line selling cigarettes and candy. A yellow policeman was there to keep the street gangs from shoving to the front. A woman my mother knew asked if she was well and how she was managing and my mother shrugged and said, 'With us, nothing's happy.'

The flour was thirty-five złotys per kilo. There was no more of the bread made from green wheat and only a few loaves made from bran and potato peelings. She bought a kilo for sixteen złotys. It was sticky but it smelled dry. She turned it over a few times in her hands. 'If they mix in too much sawdust it feels like you're eating off the street,' she said as we walked. She pressed her face to the loaf when she thought I wasn't looking. We went a few blocks before she finally packed it away in her bag. Then she thumped it twice for good luck and took my hand again and we headed home.

* * *

Our gang had trouble with another gang. They outnumbered us. We sent off two pillowcases of butter beans we stole with Zofia and Adina, but outsmarted ourselves because the other gang followed them and took the beans. They also knocked Adina down when she tried to stop them. She got up and slapped their leader's face and they kicked her.

'Aron and I are going to take care of it,' Boris told the girls.

'We are?' I said.

'You are?' Lutek said, 'Why him?'

'Because three people would be too many,' Boris said.

'Why not me?' Lutek said.

'Because it's time he did something around here,' Boris said.

'What are you going to do?' Adina asked.

'We're going to impose a tariff,' Boris said.

'What does that mean?' she wanted to know. But he said she'd find out.

The next morning he led me back to the Chłodna Street gate. 'That one's the leader,' he said, pointing out a boy in a plaid cap and braces loafing beside a family that was selling something out of a box on the street.

'How do you know?' I asked, but he ignored me. He took the jar of honey his family had brought with them out of his shirt front and handed it to me.

'When I was little I told myself that if I wasn't going to be taller than anyone else I could at least be meaner,' he said. He told me to wait a half hour and then to let the boy see the honey when I passed him and to lead him to Mirów. He said to make sure I stayed on the left side of the street coming down Mirów and if more than two of them followed me then I should take off my cap once I turned onto Elektoralna. He said not to sweat it and that I wouldn't lose a hair on my head.

'What are you going to do?' I asked.

'Shut up and carry the honey,' he said.

'We don't even know what he's like,' I told him.

'He's a bandit, like us,' he said.

I waited and then did as he said. At first I thought it hadn't worked but on Solna when I looked back I saw the kid turn towards a shop window.

On Elektoralna there were fewer people around, and even fewer on Mirów, since it was so short and led directly to the wall. Down that far there weren't any occupied buildings, only a doorway with half a sign over it standing in the ruins. I could see in a window across the street that the kid had got closer. What are you going to do when you run out of street? I wondered as I passed the doorway and saw Boris down in the rubble with a finger to his mouth and a brick in his other hand.

I turned to face the kid and he stopped but he'd already come too far and Boris swung the brick into the side of his plaid cap and knocked him to the sidewalk and then grabbed him by the shoulders and dragged him into where the cellar had fallen and no one could see us from the street. I followed him. Boris dumped him there and then picked up another brick and hit him again. It sounded like a shovel going into dirt.

'What did you *do*?' I asked. I sounded like a baby.

'Why did you turn around?' he said. He seemed angrier at me than at the kid.

'Is he dead?' I asked. But I could see that he wasn't. His head was jerking back and forth and his hands were clenching.

Boris squatted and pulled out a safetypin and a note that said LIVE AND LET LIVE and pinned it to the kid's shirt.

'Give me the honey,' he said. Then he pulled me back onto the street.

'We're just going to leave him?' I asked. But we already had.

That afternoon we had Chłodna Street to ourselves. Boris said the other gang was probably still out looking for its leader. We used ten or twelve smaller kids to swarm the gate. They went off shoulder to shoulder running as fast as they could and the blue and yellow police beat and tore at the clothes of as many as they could reach, but most got through. We paid each a saccharine candy and told them to wait until the gate was at its busiest, Boris found the whole thing funny. He said that because we'd been paid in money for a recent load he was going to have us split up and buy things in Aryan shops outside the wall. He said the trick was to walk slowly and to pass the police as though they were vendors and not to run even if someone made a first step at us. And to clean our clothes and shoes as much as we could before we left. And when we were in the shops to ask for what we wanted as though we owned the place.

'How's your sister?' Adina asked Zofia, and I slapped my head for not having asked her myself.

Zofia said Salcia was doing poorly. Adina wrapped an arm around her and Zofia asked if she was getting sick and Adina told her that two more families had moved into their apartment. And while those families had been sitting and chatting with one of their uncles another had arrived. She had no idea where they were going to put them all. 'Now we're six to a room,' she said. 'And in the cellar and in one corner the water's always dripping. Next to my head, all night long. We asked them to fix it but they didn't fix it.'

In the square one of the blue policemen had a kid by the shirt and tore it off his back. 'Did you cut yourself?' Zofia asked me.

'He has bad gums,' Boris told her. 'Have you smelled his breath?'

So I told them what Boris had done.

'With a brick?' Lutek said when I finished.

'On the head,' I said.

'Hooray for Boris,' Adina said.

'I think he's dead,' I said.

'He should've realized stealing is wrong,' Boris said.

'Do you think they'll leave us alone now?' Zofia asked.

'If they don't they'll get another brick to the head,' Boris told her.

'Hooray for Boris,' Adina said.

'You already said that,' Lutek told her. And then I understood why Boris had used me instead of Lutek.

'He might really be dead,' I said again, but they all looked like they had their own problems.

'Why are we still sitting here?' Adina wanted to know.

'We're waiting for confirmation from the other side,' Boris told her. We had to move an exchange location and had sent one of the smaller kids with a note.

I asked Zofia if her father was still sad about the Brysz girls.

'What do you care?' she said.

'I asked, didn't I?' I said.

'Poor Sh'maya,' Boris said. 'No one thinks he cares.'

She said her father was better but that Hanka Nasielska still wept night and day about it. 'Hanka Nasielska saw me with you and called me treyf slops in a treyf pot,' she told Boris. He laughed.

'What were you doing with him?' I asked.

'She told me she'd make my mouth kosher again,' she said to Boris. 'She put a stone in a pot with some steam but I screamed that it was too hot so she cooled it down before she put it back in my mouth.'

'So that's how you make a mouth kosher?' Boris asked.

Zofia looked away and wiped her eyes and Adina punched his arm. 'There's not one good Jew among us,' Zofia said.

'The good Jews buy what we bring in,' Boris said.

'What about your brother?' Adina asked.

'What about yours?' Zofia said. 'The oldest one.'

'He prays by himself on weekdays and goes to the public services on holidays,' Adina said. 'When they have them. Weren't your uncles religious?'

Zofia said one uncle went to shul but didn't daven and just sat there, and that the other didn't even go to shul. Though he always tried to get them a carp or goose for the Sabbath.

A kid who hadn't got through the gate started to come over for his saccharine candy but Boris warned him away with his eyes.

'Sh'maya here had only four people move in with him,' Adina said bitterly. 'We had a village move in with us.'

'It could've been a lot worse for his family,' Boris told her. 'I had six brothers and sisters and five of them died as babies.'

'Your poor mother,' Zofia said.

'And look at the son who lived,' Lutek said.

'I used to tell my mother I was afraid I wouldn't have children,' Zofia said. 'She used to tell me not to say that and that I'd have children; I'd see.'

'Maybe this year,' Boris said. Lutek laughed.

'Where I come from the girls are tough but not smart,' Adina said. 'For a while I thought from a kiss you could get pregnant.'

'From mine you can,' Boris said. Lutek and Adina made fun of him for boasting.

'It's a miracle I'm normal,' Zofia said. 'If I *am* normal.'

'You're not,' Lutek told her.

'I know *you're* not,' she told him.

A work detail came back through the gate, It took a half hour for everyone's papers to be checked at all three guard posts. Neither of our fathers were in the group. Neither of my brothers were either.

'Did you ever act in the holiday plays in kheyder?' Adina asked Boris. When she saw his look she said she was just asking.

'What's wrong with you?' he wanted to know.

The kid who'd had his shirt torn off was shrieking in the square from the beating he'd received. Where he was squatting the traffic had to go around him. He was trying to reach the part of his back that hurt.

'Enough already with the noise,' Lutek said. The kid's shrieking turned to weeping and he crouched around in the dust without standing up.

'I'll see what's going on,' Boris finally said. He stood and crossed the street to the pharmacy.

'Where's he going?' Adina asked.

'From the second floor you can see over the wall,' Lutek told her.

After a few minutes Boris came back and flopped down so his feet went up into the air. 'He's over there,' he said. 'I don't know what he's waiting for.'

The squatting kid finally stood up and headed over to us like a little cripple.

'Just what we need,' Boris said.

'Give me my candy,' the kid said when he stopped in front of us. No one at the guard posts was paying attention.

'Give him his candy,' Boris told Zofia. She handed him a piece from a little sack in the waistband of her skirt.

'I should get two,' the kid said. He had a lazy eye that made him even uglier.

'Why should you get two?' Boris asked him.

'Because I took such a beating,' the kid said.

'Well, I should have a roast goose,' Lutek told him. 'But we don't always get what we want.'

'I should get two,' the kid repeated.

'Get away from us or we'll show you what a beating looks like,' Boris told him.

'I'll call the police,' the kid said.

Boris stood up and lifted him off his feet by the neck with one hand.

'What are you doing there? Put him down,' someone shouted, scaring us.

It was Korczak, the Old Doctor. 'You should be *ashamed*,' he said. He pulled Boris's arm from the kid's neck. Zofia and Adina got to their feet.

'Get out of here, Grandfather,' Boris told him. 'I can smell the vodka.'

The old man straightened up. I couldn't smell it. Then he said, 'Pay attention. What I have to say may come in handy.'

'This is the Old Doctor,' Adina told Boris. 'He runs the orphanage.'

The old man waited, as though that was going to change something.

'So did you come to lecture us or do you have a suggestion to make?' Boris said.

'I have a suggestion to make,' Korczak said. 'I suggest you leave my boys alone. I suggest you leave *all* these boys alone.'

'Who made you King of the World?' Lutek said.

'I'm sorry for our friends,' Zofia told him.

'Mietek, go home,' Korczak said to the kid. The kid moved behind him. They made quite the pair: the old man with dirty spectacles and the shirtless kid with the lazy eye.

'You have pants like a hobo's,' Boris said.

'A hobo wouldn't take them,' Korczak told him.

'You know where I found him?' Boris said, nodding at the kid. 'Looking through the rubbish. Maybe you should feed your kids.'

'Anyone who's got in my way can tell you I can still kick pretty hard,' Korczak told him.

'This old wreck's *threatening* me?' Boris asked Zofia.

'Boris, let's go,' Adina told him.

'Did we make you do anything, kid?' Boris asked.

'You don't care what happens,' Korczak

told him. 'Or who gets hurt. Just so in the meantime you can find a piece of bread somewhere. Right?'

'You're the big shot with your own place, judging us?' Boris said.

'Our own place? What does a Jew have?' Korczak told him. 'We've never owned a thing.'

'So maybe the houses are theirs,' Boris told him. 'But the streets are ours.'

'The streets are yours?' Korczak said. 'Look around.'

'We do all right,' Boris said.

'Leave my boys alone,' Korczak repeated.

'Go back to your orphanage,' Boris told him. 'Dish out some soup.'

The old man turned to the rest of us. 'For each one who acts like that, there's another who behaves decently,' he said. Then he left, holding the kid by the shoulder. And the kid we'd been waiting for finally made it through the gate to let us know that our new arrangement was going to be okay.

* * *

Every morning my mother begged me to go to the Order Service headquarters to see what information Lejkin would give me. Sometimes I waited till noon before he would see me. He told me that my father and one brother were still together and that they'd worked in the SS barracks in Rakowiecka Street, in the cavalry barracks at Służewiec, and spreading coal bricks at a railroad siding outside of town. He said he thought they'd also done some road construction. They hadn't been paid for it yet since the Judenrat was behind in its wages, but they had been given bread and radishes. He thought they were in a camp in the Kampinos forest. My other brother and Boris's father he knew nothing about. He said families whose main breadwinner had been selected for the camps were eligible for a small welfare payment from the Judenrat, though he wasn't sure whom to see about that. He also said that since I was now thirteen it was time for me to be registered as well. I left this out of what I reported to my mother.

He said he had little information beyond that. Czerniaków himself had personally intervened about the state of the camps with the SS man in charge of Jewish affairs and the director of the Department of Jewish Labor in the Arbeitsamt, and both more food and better conditions had been promised.

One morning in a downpour I opened our door and Lejkin was standing there in the hall with an SS officer behind him. The officer was tall and had a sou'wester on his cap. He smiled and shook the water from the arms of his raincoat and moved Lejkin aside with his hand and said, 'Guten Morgen.' He sounded like someone who was happy that he'd kept his patience for so long with misbehaving children. He asked in Polish if I spoke German. When I told him no he nodded and wiped the mud from his boots so energetically that he split our old doormat in two.

The left sleeve of his uniform jacket was tucked into his belt and there was no arm in it. He saw me looking and said in Polish, 'Wars aren't much fun. Now don't you feel like a lucky young boy?'

Lejkin introduced him as Obersturmführer Witossek. I said hello and the German seemed amused by my tone.

Boris pretended to be asleep on the floor near my feet. 'I'd ask to come in but perhaps now is not the best time,' the German said.

'His Polish is good, isn't it?' Lejkin asked.

'You're Aron Różycki?' the German asked.

'Yes,' I told him.

'Could you step into the hall,' he said.

'Aron!' my mother called from the kitchen.

I stepped out and he shut the door behind me. The window in the hallway was broken and it made the rain louder. A family camped under it had strung up a shelter to keep dry, A bucket caught the runoff.

The German said he wanted me to come to an office he was setting up Żelazna Street. A dozen Jews were already there, and Lejkin had recommended me.

What was I supposed to do at such a place, I wanted to know.

'It's a little Jewish concern,' he said. 'Your friend here is part of it. He's the one who recommended you,' he repeated.

'Recommended me for what?' I said.

'Well, there's always more to discover when you stick your nose into the world,' he said. I looked at Lejkin, who raised his shoulders.

'Or you can serve in a labor battalion,' the German said. 'Do you have your card?'

'I'm not registered yet,' I said.

'It's 103 Żelazna,' the German said. 'Your friend can tell you if there's anything else you need to know.'

'There isn't anything else you need to know,' Lejkin said.

'Oh, and yes,' the German said as he was leaving. He opened the door and there inside the apartment stood my mother and Boris's mother, gaping. 'Could I ask you for some sort of Jewish holy volume or object?'

We looked at one another. 'An object?' Boris's mother said.

'Something in which you believe,' the German said.

'Something in which they believe?' Lejkin said.

'To serve as a charm,' the German said. While we still stood there, he added, 'I had one before from Cologne and you can see what happened when I lost it.'

Boris's mother left the doorway. My mother just stared. 'Good morning,' the German said to her.

'Good morning,' she answered.

Boris's mother returned with a mezuzah that she handed to the German.

'Thank you,' the German said, once he had it. 'Auf wiedersehen.'

★ ★ ★

Boris spent an entire day happy because one of our contacts over the wall told him that so much bread was being smuggled into the ghetto there was an actual shortage of it on the other side. Lutek's old chiseled passage in the wall on Przejazd Street had been bricked up and reopened so often that people started calling it the Immortal Hole. The Germans cleared away the shed that covered it. Boris said that the hole proved there were only three invincible forces in the universe: the

German Army, the British Navy, and Jewish smuggling.

The guards at Chłodna Street developed a new money-making scheme of announcing at twenty minutes to the hour that it was already curfew and charging twenty złotys apiece to fix their watches to the correct time and send you on your way, so we went back to the Immortal Hole. Boris worked out a schedule with the other gangs that let us use it right before and after curfew. We went through and did our buying and selling in pairs, and if we didn't see the next pair behind us we didn't wait for them.

In bad weather Zofia went through with her shoes around her neck and the laces tied together, She said her shoes actually fitted her and if she ruined them she'd never find another pair that did.

Boris hadn't mentioned the German or Lejkin after they'd left and he ignored how upset my mother was about it, but after four days he stopped me as we went downstairs and asked if I was just going to act as if nothing had happened. I asked what he was talking about.

'Do you think they're just going to forget you?' he said. 'Do you really want to piss in that one-armed German's beer?'

'I was going to go,' I told him.

'Try not to always be so stupid,' he said. 'These are the people with the whip hand. These are the people who are going to have information first.'

'What information?' I said.

'Whatever information there is,' he said. 'Where the jumps will be, what gates will play, what players will be there, who they're going to move against and when.'

'I know that,' I told him.

'Use your head,' he said.

'I said I was going,' I said.

'Then go,' he said. 'Don't stand here with me.'

But Lejkin wasn't there and no one knew what to do with me. I was told to wait in the hall. It was a big fancy house so the floor was marble. Everyone's steps echoed. Yellow police came and went but the only Jew who introduced himself was a shoeshine boy named Ajzyk. He sat opposite me in the front hall along with a few rickshaw drivers who took Germans around the ghetto. All morning laborers carried in what looked like an entire kitchen, and in the afternoon a barber's chair and other crates and boxes as well. I had no breakfast and asked if there was anything to eat but no one answered. Twice more I went in to ask what was happening and was told to wait. The fourth time I presented myself I was told to come back the next day. Then going down the steps I ran into Lejkin, who said I should come back Friday.

★ ★ ★

The next time we got to the Immortal Hole a German soldier was standing in front of it while a Jew in a smock unloaded a handcart filled with metal sheets. The building alongside had a slanted roof with dormers that hid you from the street so we went up to watch. We'd found the spot a week earlier. You got there through a hatch on the ceiling of the caretaker's closet on the top floor. We could all fit between the dormers and every so often one of us could keep an eye on what was going on below.

The tradesman held the sheets over the hole and pounded in masonry nails. His hammer on the metal was so loud that Zofia put her fingers in her ears.

'Those will pull right out,' Boris said after he took a look. He had one of his cigarettes going. He collected them off the streets and used a pin to smoke them down to the very end.

'This breeze is nice,' Adina said.

We stayed up there to celebrate Zofia's

birthday. Lutek said he'd be thirteen soon too and Adina had made each of us write Zofia a note with good wishes and give her a present. Zofia read each note that was handed over, then folded it into the sack in her waistband. Mine said *You Are the Kindest Person I Know* and *Thank You For Making Us Happier.*

Then came our gifts. Boris gave her candied cherries in a folded packet of newspaper. Lutek gave her a scarf with the constellations. Adina gave her a tin of jam. I gave her a miniature black book that said *My Diary* on the front.

Zofia thanked us and said we should share the cherries and that this was one of her best birthdays ever. 'I know that's hard to believe,' she said.

She said when she was young and they still lived in their nice apartment her mother hadn't let her play with other children in their courtyard, so instead she'd had to content herself one birthday with going out on her balcony and tossing down cutouts and handmade toys and calling out, 'Here, you kids, take these!' and watching them play. And one kid had written in chalk *Zofia is crazy* on their stairwell.

'That's a nice birthday,' Adina said, then asked again how Salcia was, and Zofia said that she might do better if they could cheer her up somehow. She'd left her favorite stuffed bear behind when they moved to the ghetto because while she didn't know where they were going she knew it would be a bad place.

'Well, that's another good birthday story,' Lutek finally said.

'She has another bear now,' Zofia told him.

Adina said that she got caught on her last birthday. A Polish woman had grabbed her on the Aryan side and had told the whole street that she had a Jewish nose. Zofia asked what happened then, and Adina said no one had cared and that Adina had answered, 'What kind of nose do *you* have? Look at yourself in the mirror!' and that had made the woman let go and run away.

Lutek said he was hungry. Zofia said now when her family finished their soup her brother Leon put the pot over his head so he could lick the bottom clean.

Adina said people in France cooked potatoes in oil, not water, and Zofia said oil-fried potatoes must taste amazing and Boris said that was probably true but good oil could be put to better use.

Boris and I looked back over the edge of the gutter. The Jew with the smock had finished and he and the German soldier had left and one of the other gangs was already around the hole. A kid with a crowbar levered the metal sheet away from the brick and the masonry nails came out as easily as Boris said they would. The sheet was bent aside but then a German officer and three yellow policemen appeared like magic. When two kids tried to scramble through the hole there were shouts on the other side and they were dragged back. They all lined up against the wall on the German officer's orders. He had only one arm.

'That's him,' Boris said.

'I know,' I told him.

Witossek told them each to hand over their money and after counting it he said that he was going to fine them that amount for smuggling. They stood along the wall. He caught sight of an old Jew hurrying across the street a block away and called him over. One of the yellow police had to cross over to get him to come. We could see him trembling from where we were.

'How old are you?' Witossek asked. Sixty-six, the old Jew told him and Witossek counted out sixty-six złotys and stuffed them in the old man's shirt pocket. 'Now be on your way,' he said.

He said something else to the same yellow policeman, who walked off and came back with three other Jews. Witossek asked their ages and paid them that amount of złotys. The last woman said she was fifty and he counted out his last forty-eight złotys and said that was now her age instead. Once she left he turned to the smugglers and said, 'I'm a good German, aren't I?' They said he was and he led his yellow policemen away and as soon as he was out of their sight the three of them scattered.

★ ★ ★

On Friday I waited again for three hours and then Ajzyk the shoeshine boy came out and told me that Lejkin said I should come back on Monday. On Monday Lejkin finally showed me into his office, which was a room next to the toilet. He spread his arms like he was taking in all of Poland and asked what I thought. I told him the house had a nice front hall.

He said Witossek and other Germans in the Security Police were putting together an anti-crime unit and that Lejkin had picked me to be a part of it. 'They're not hunting smugglers as much as wanting to regulate them,' he said. 'You know how the Germans like to keep track of everything.'

'I don't know anything about anything,' I said.

'Yes, that's been your position,' he told me. 'But you do know the old joke that's now going around again. If two Jews meet, one says to the other, 'Statistically, one of us must be reporting to the Gestapo!''

'I have heard that joke,' I told him.

'There's no salary, of course, but there are other advantages,' he said. 'Including influence in the work camps.'

'I still don't even know what I'm supposed to do,' I said.

'Nothing for the time being,' he said. 'Maybe some minor reports. Maybe not even that.'

I sat in my chair and he looked at me. He was so small behind his desk that it looked like he was kneeling on the floor. I could hear an accordion player outside his window.

'So can I go now?' I asked.

'No,' he said.

He gave his attention to some papers in front of him. He signed two and made a mocking noise at a third. He stood up and came around the front of his desk and said he'd traded for new boots, then walked around and did knee bends to break them in.

'Have you heard that the Germans are already in Leningrad?' he asked. I shook my head.

'So Hitler sees Jesus in Paradise and says to

St Peter, 'Hey, what's that Jew doing without an armband?'' he said. 'And St Peter tells him, 'Leave him alone. He's the Boss's son.''

'That's a good joke,' I told him, after we were quiet for a while.

'You're like those shopkeepers who hold goods under their coats and go over to customers only when they recognize them,' he said, 'I like that about you.'

'Thank you,' I said.

'We have to stick together,' he told me. 'It's a terrible thing to see how the Germans have divided us.'

'So can I go now?' I said.

'Do you remember how you felt the first time you saw a Jews Not Wanted sign in the window of a Jewish shop?' he said.

Another policeman swung the door open and told Lejkin that one of the Czapliński brothers was finally there. Lejkin tossed him two packs of cigarettes and the policeman said that the Czaplińskis smoked too, Lejkin tossed him two more. 'Weren't they both lawyers, as well?' the policeman wanted to know.

'I think they were, yes,' Lejkin told him. 'Back in Lódz.'

'It's like a bar association around here,' the policeman said. He said that Mayler was a lawyer too and by the way he was still trying to find out where his wife's family had been

131

sent. 'The Poles complain that we're privileged because they all got sent abroad and we at least got to work at home,' he told Lejkin.

'Tell the Organ Grinders,' Lejkin told him, and the policeman left.

'Who are the Organ Grinders?' I asked.

'That's what they call the Judenrat,' he said. 'You know: throw a coin to the organ grinder and he plays along with his monkey.'

He bent to fix his boots and once he was happy with them went back behind his desk and sat down again. 'So what's your decision?' he said.

We both listened to the minute hand of his clock click over into the next position. 'I think I'll do what I can to help,' I told him.

He said I'd be hearing from him and dismissed me. When I was heading down the front steps a long black car pulled up with two Germans in the front and three bearded Jews with terrified eyes in the back. When I told Boris that evening he clapped me on the back for having done the smart thing and said maybe now we'd get some word in advance as to what was going on.

* * *

Hanka Nasielska got the typhus and died. So did Zofia's Uncle Ickowicz. For a few weeks

Lejkin passed along messages from my father and brother and then he said they'd been transferred and he didn't know where. My mother asked me to find out and told me to spend more time with him until I did. There were more soup kitchens on the street. In September Lejkin said the ghetto would be further reduced in size but that in October some schools could open again. He had our gang hang some new placards forbidding Jews from leaving the housing districts designated for them.

'What does it mean?' Zofia asked the day we got them, though after we finished hanging them we found out: German soldiers and blue police surprised us at the Immortal Hole and the gang got away but a Pole grabbed me by the back of the neck. Three older kids from another gang also were caught. The Pole gave me a kick in the behind, let me go, and said, 'This one's too short to shoot.' The other kids were told to empty their pockets and stand against the wall. I ran away and after I rounded the corner I heard them shooting. Later the dead kids were still there on top of one another against the wall.

★ ★ ★

Going home from a shop with my mother we heard more shots and she dragged me to the pavement and covered me with her arm. At dinner she told us that four bodies had been found beside the wall at Nowolipke.

'A lot of people have typhus,' Boris said.

She told him they'd been shot for smuggling.

'That's why we're not going to do that anymore,' he told her.

'Is that the truth?' she asked me.

'We already decided not to,' I told her.

Boris told her smuggling had got too dangerous and that a housepainter on his way to a job had been ordered by a German to fill in the Immortal Hole one more time and then when that German wandered off, another came along and, seeing a Jew working on a hole in the wall, shot him dead. Boris's mother asked what the Immortal Hole was and we told her.

Two days later it was open again. We gave up on it but heard that a German with a bullhorn had announced to the neighborhood that thirty Jews would be shot if it wasn't permanently closed by noon the next day. We also heard the smuggling went on as before after he left and that he never came back.

* * *

Boris got caught. He said that when they were about to shoot him a cloud of gnats flew into his eyes and nose and also bothered the Germans, who argued with one another while he stood there against the wall and then for whatever reason just left him there.

Adina and Zofia embraced him and Lutek said he'd had some close scrapes of his own and the only reason he hadn't been killed was he was so short that all the bullets went over his head.

Zofia said, 'I think we have to stop.'

And Boris said, 'What's the difference how you're done for? You have to eat.'

'It's time to think of something else,' Adina told him.

'Yes,' Boris said, as if he were talking to small children. 'Let's do that.'

We liked to meet outside Mrs Melecówna's matrimonial introductions parlor because she let young people in the courtyard and it had an awning besides. One morning Adina and Boris and I waited an hour before Lutek finally arrived. He was sweating so much from running that the bill of his cap was soaked through. He said Zofia had popped up at his window at midnight the night before. Her family had been getting ready for bed when they heard boots on the stairs, which was always bad news after curfew. Her mother tucked Zofia and Leon into a space she'd made under the bedframe before going to the door. The Germans searched but had been distracted by all of the valises they'd dragged out from under the bed and emptied. Zofia and Leon didn't make a sound though they heard Salcia crying and Jechiel and their father protesting and their father telling the Germans about his broom factory. Their mother told the Germans, 'I'm coming, I'm coming,' as if saying goodbye to Zofia and Leon. They stayed quiet after everyone left, climbed out, and then in the street walked into more Germans. While they were being chased she shouted to Leon to run in one direction and she'd go in another and he was shouting back, 'Why should I run that way?' when the Germans caught him. She spent the night weeping that this had been the last thing he'd said to her.

Adina asked Lutek why she'd gone to his apartment and Boris reminded her it was the closest. Adina said we had to go to her but Lutek said she wasn't there anyway, that his father had already made her leave. Who knew why the Germans wanted them, or how hard they'd look? He'd walked her over to an old friend of her mother's, who took her in without enthusiasm.

I spent three days working as a peeler in a

communal kitchen with my mother and then Adina said Zofia wanted to see me. She gave me the address and said she'd already visited and that the family was gone all day at a shoemaking factory and Zofia said I should ring the bell three times and then stand in the street where she could see me.

The apartment had a washbasin in the sink and a rabbit hutch that was locked with a padlock on a high wardrobe.

'The mother puts the bread up there so I can't get to it at night when they're sleeping,' Zofia said. 'I just stand here smelling it in the dark.'

'They don't feed you?' I asked.

'I'm so hungry I suck on my knee,' she said. She said that they gave her food like for a dog. She said Boris had brought the family some kasha for her and that the family ate it instead in front of her.

I told her we could bring her more food. She said she helped with the chores and always tried to be calm and quiet and grown-up but found herself waiting for her mother to come and take her away. She was trying not to always be weeping. She asked me to find out through my friend in the yellow police where her family had been taken.

'He's not my friend,' I told her.

'Please,' she said, then said she kept thinking about how brave Leon had been. She said you couldn't believe the thunder of the Germans once they were in a room.

At first Lejkin told me he had no information but when I wouldn't leave him alone he said he'd see what he could find out and the next day he told me they'd been sent to the country as part of a new initiative and wouldn't be coming back; they were to be resettled out there. Adina told Zofia, whose response was that she was going to go to them and we all needed to help her get out of the ghetto as soon as possible.

Boris surprised us by saying we should help her and Lutek asked what was so hard, we went through all the time, and Boris told him the difficulty was in getting far enough away to avoid the blackmailers. In the meantime she had to find a new place since her mother's friend was starving her. Boris found it in a day and Adina took her there when the street traffic was the busiest.

The day before she was to leave we all went to say goodbye. The woman whose apartment it was asked us to visit one at a time so as not to attract attention. Boris went first. Adina said she wanted to go last and Lutek said he didn't need to go at all.

A woman in a red flowered robe let me in

and then shut herself in the bathroom. Zofia was wearing three layers of clothes and her shoes that fitted. She tried to keep her hands in her lap but they kept flying around. She said this woman had German visitors and so Zofia hid in a recess behind the toilet in a stored washtub. She said that of course the Germans used the toilet all the time.

I asked if everything was ready and she said that Boris had found a man who said because she had better looks he would give her money to get herself and his daughter out of the ghetto. I asked what she meant by better and she said as in not like a Jew.

She said the man's wife had scrubbed her in a tub and had to change the water three times. She said the man had said his daughter could pass for Zofia's sister. She said that he was providing papers for both of them and that they'd almost left two days earlier. He'd led them into the cellar of a pharmacy that bordered the Aryan side where they were supposed to wait for someone, but no one came. She said the new plan was that a wagon driver would pull up with his cart at dawn and stuff them under some bedding and drive them through the gate.

'Don't go,' I said, while she was still talking. 'Stay with us.'

She was surprised by how upset I was. 'I

139

shouldn't try to find my family?' she said.

'Who knows if that's really where they are?' I said.

'Well, if they're not there, where are they?' she asked. She stared like I was refusing to tell her.

'You don't know anybody on the other side,' I said.

She said she did. When I asked who, she wouldn't answer. Then she said some of the kids in the newer gangs were from the youth movements that left when the Germans marched in.

'Why are they coming back?' I asked.

'To help,' she said.

'With what?' I asked.

'You don't need to know,' she said. 'And don't pull such a face. But they have contacts on the other side.'

I asked if the kid she called Antek was one of the ones she was talking about. She was annoyed I'd noticed, but then said that he was. We sat there like two strangers at a puppet show.

'Do you have to go?' I said again.

She looked at me like I'd said something shameful. 'So I should leave Leon wherever he is?' she said. 'And Salcia? And my mother?' I didn't answer.

'I spend my whole life around people who

don't ask me about myself,' she added. She said she was surprised by how much this disappointed her.

'Do you know what I'm talking about?' she asked me. When I again didn't answer, she said I should go get Adina.

'Why? You're finished with me?' I said.

'Oh, Aron,' she said tiredly.

'What?' I said.

'You're a good boy,' she said. 'Take care of yourself.' She took my hands and squeezed them.

On the stairs I stopped and turned to go back but decided it wouldn't be a good idea since I wasn't the same person I used to be and she wouldn't have liked me even then.

⋆　⋆　⋆

That night my mother was surprised when I climbed into bed with her after everyone else had fallen asleep. She smelled like cabbage and the coal from the stove. 'Did you have a bad dream?' she said in her sleepy voice. Her finger tickled my ear.

'Don't cry,' I told her, and she tucked my head under her chin. She called me her beautiful boy when I put my arms around her neck. When I woke in the morning I'd wet the bed.

'Tit for tat, my friend,' Lejkin told me when I came out onto the street. I was looking for Boris, who'd got up ahead of me. 'I helped you; you have to help me.'

He wanted to know what we had planned for the day. He said he had his quotas to fill, too. I told him I didn't know what he meant and he said that he was getting tired of everything I didn't know and could I just answer the question. So I told him where we were likely to be and he thanked me and left and an hour later two blue policemen caught Lutek and me with a burlap sack of turnips and threw us and the turnips into the back of a car.

They drove us to a big building with tall columns outside of the ghetto and took us down into the cellar. A German soldier at a desk asked what they were bringing him and they told him they had two for the Streetcar. We were walked down a long dark corridor and pushed into a room with cement walls and no windows.

There were two rows of hard wooden seats with arms along the walls facing forward like a little classroom and I sat in one and Lutek sat in another behind a tall man with a bloody head and wild hair. The walls were covered in scratched graffiti. Next to my bench someone had carved JEZU. Next to

Lutek's someone had drawn a clock and circled the 6. I wasn't afraid but I was shaking as though I'd been left out in the cold.

Lutek asked the tall man where we were. He told us this was Gestapo headquarters and they called this room the Streetcar because of its shape and that we should ask for coffee when the woman in uniform came past.

She walked by a few minutes later and Lutek asked her and she came back with a mug of coffee with milk in it and passed it to him through the bars. He shared it with the man with the bloody head.

'You're shaking your whole chair,' he said to me.

He said Boris had told him he'd been here once and found himself in the same cell with the guy who'd pointed him out to some Germans on the street.

'What did he do?' I asked.

'What do you think?' Lutek said.

'It was like they were waiting for us,' he said a few minutes later. When I didn't say anything, he said, 'Did you hear what I said? It was like they knew we were coming.'

'Do you think once they talk to us they'll let us go?' I whispered.

'How would I know?' he said.

He asked if Lejkin had any more war news.

I told him no. He said he heard the Germans were taking a beating outside Moscow and Leningrad. The man with the bloody head told him to be quiet. Lutek told him the joke that when Napoleon invaded Russia he put on a red tunic in case he was wounded, and Hitler put on brown pants. The man with the bloody head got up and moved as far away as he could.

Finally two German soldiers appeared with a list. They mispronounced our names but we raised our hands. They took us out into a courtyard in the back without windows. One soldier took Lutek by the shoulders and pushed his back against the wall.

We couldn't tell if they understood Polish. Lutek said to them, 'Are you really going to kill me over some turnips?' and the German who'd pushed him shot him. His head hit the wall so hard that his rabbit-skin cap landed on the dirt in front of him. Because of his wooden shoes each foot skidded out from under him in a different direction. The other German was so upset by the noise I made that he knocked me to the ground. The two of them picked me up and carried me back through the waiting hall past the rooms with the benches and threw me out onto the street.

★ ★ ★

On my way home my legs acted like I kept forgetting how to walk and I stopped in the center of the road. I threw my own cap away. A truck honked and someone finally dragged me to the curb.

Three or four times a day my mother asked what was wrong. After a few days she told Boris's mother there was nothing for her to do but to keep her shoulder to the plow until she fell on her face. Boris's mother said that was all anyone could do. Boris asked me where Lutek had disappeared to and I told him I didn't know. His sister was always weeping and he told her to shut up from where he was lying on the floor. She rubbed her crippled hand, which was what she did to calm herself. My mother made a new project of painting the beds with turpentine and ammonia to kill the bedbugs but stayed sad that I wouldn't talk with her. 'Someday you'll wish you had,' she said.

One night I got up and sat with her in the kitchen. She blew on the fire in the stove and waved a rag near the open grate and watched me scratch at my lice. When I was finished she asked if I was hungry. I asked if there was anything she could do about that and she said no.

Boris's mother said from her pallet in the dark she'd heard that the refugees were taking over the apartments of those who starved to death or died of the typhus. She said that with the cold they invaded any place they could and chopped and burned whatever furniture they found. My mother said that nowadays they took the roof away from over your head the minute you turned your back.

And who was to stop them? Boris's mother wanted to know.

No one should look for heroes on our street, my mother told her.

I told her not to get herself worked up and she told me that I always wanted to know why she was so upset and meanwhile here we all were, with everyone either dying or waiting their turn. Boris snickered from the hallway.

She said she wasn't a young woman and that if it wasn't for my sake she wouldn't have had the strength to do this.

Do what? Boris wanted to know. Keep us all awake?

She said my still being here with her was beshert. Did I know what beshert meant?

I didn't, I told her. I was tired of her talking.

Beshert meant 'meant to be,' she said. She said *she* knew I needed her, even if I didn't. She was wearing the nightshirt my father liked, though it wasn't as warm, in case he came home in the middle of the night. I

146

wiped my eyes so hard I blinded myself at first.

'Why do you act like this?' Boris's mother said from her pallet. 'Do you think your mother needs this now?'

'Shut up, all of you,' Boris said. When his sister whimpered he said, 'You shut up too.'

My mother and I watched the embers in the stove through the grate. 'I work and I worry,' she said. 'That's what I do.'

'I'm sorry,' I told her.

'I know,' she said and then told me I should try to sleep.

I didn't see Boris for a day and then he came home and stood in front of me, enraged. I asked where he'd been and he knocked me down with a forearm to my face. That night he threw my sleeping pallet into my mother's room. She asked what was going on and I climbed into her bed.

She fell down the next morning when she tried to wash herself near the stove and we couldn't get her up. At first Boris wouldn't help but then finally we carried her to the hospital and a doctor who was sick himself told her she'd got the typhus she'd been waiting for. She passed out after he told her. They put her on a bed in the hallway and another patient beside her told her the news about America having entered the war. Her

147

reaction disappointed him. She had such a fever I could feel the heat standing next to her and her chills were so bad the other sick people moved their beds farther away. While I sat with her she wept and tried to keep covered up and apologized for the smell. Her diarrhea meant she had to keep getting up and she no longer had the energy to fully clean herself. She said she didn't want me to catch anything and told me to leave and then asked me to stay. I told her she'd probably caught what she had from me.

They moved her to the quarantine ward and left her on a pallet in another hallway. No one gave her medicine. I was told I couldn't stay but no one noticed I hadn't left. A woman holding her baby shouted, 'This is supposed to be a hospital! I should burn it down!' Her baby's face was blue.

We were outside a separate quarantine room for children. When I looked in they never moved their hands but just lay there in their beds.

She wanted me to make sure Boris and his mother knew which hospital it was so my father and brothers would know where to find us. She sent me home to tell them. She told me to stay there but I went back and forth when she slept. They served her blood soup she liked and spit soup she didn't. It was spit soup because it used unthreshed grain and the husks had to be spit out.

She was sick for ten days. 'I was sad, I thought only of myself, I let you support me,' she told me on one of the days. 'The holidays again,' she complained on another, I didn't know what she was talking about. Her fever got bad and then better and then bad again. She asked if I had any good memories and I told her I did. She asked me to tell her some. I told about things I remembered from before we moved to the city. I told her I remembered a picnic in the woods with blackbirds around me in the thick grass and her standing over me and making a shadow for me in the bright sunlight. She said she knew what happened on the streets and that she saw it for herself. 'You get like a little animal,' she said. 'You lie, you cheat.'

I asked to see the doctor who'd told her she had the typhus and a nurse said he'd died. My mother was moved to another hallway on another floor and no one said why. 'I wanted to be nusik,' she told me. She wiped her cheeks on the pillow to cool her face. She asked if I knew what nusik was, and when I told her I didn't she said that it was something good. Someone useful and smart. She said that if she'd been nusik, then people who couldn't get along, people with problems, would have come to her. She would have listened. She would have contributed more than she had.

She stayed sick and the weather stayed windy and sleeting. The Hanukkah decorations fell over in the drafts from the door. She had more trouble breathing. Sometimes I slept under her bed but they found me and drove me downstairs so then I slept near the front doors under the portrait of the hospital's founder.

'You're like me,' she said one night after her breathing got so bad it woke us up. 'You think if you stay quiet you'll be able to keep going like everyone else.' She sounded so bad I found a nurse who brought her some beet marmalade and a glass of undiluted spirits.

The spirits made her cheeks red. She raised her eyebrows after a few sips as if she'd been given a treat. She asked if I wanted any. I told her that the first glassful was for her. She nodded. By then she was having such trouble breathing it sounded like she was whinnying.

She asked if I was sorry to have to go on without her. She asked if I thought I could do it. I looked into her face and wondered if she was really going to leave me. The thought made me so mad that I told her I could do anything and she set the glass of spirits on the floor and tried to sit up and I couldn't tell from her expression how bad she felt or if this made it any better.

She said the light hurt her eyes so I went down the hall and switched it off. Some of the patients on the beds and the nurse sitting at the end of the hallway with her paperwork complained, but in the dark I could see my family again, my father in his white holiday shirt and my mother and my brothers and even my younger brother, all of their faces at that point blind to what was coming.

On my walk home the streets were very bad and icy. I slipped and fell more than once. It was after curfew but there was no moon and no one wanted to be out in the cold so no one saw me. I walked like I was part of my own funeral procession. At home I let myself in and stopped, as if there were nothing for me to do and nowhere for me to go in the face of the pictures in my head.

★　★　★

I woke on my mother's blanket to the shriek of a window wrenched open and in the kitchen Boris was throwing my clothes into the street. There'd been a knock on the door and he'd answered it but I hadn't bothered to see who it was.

I stood in my nightshirt, blinking, my feet

cold on the floor. His mother and sister were also in the doorway to their room.

'Leave him alone,' his sister said when she saw me. 'His mother just died.'

'And now we're quarantined,' Boris shouted. I thought he was about to kill me, like somebody might cross a street. 'Do you know how much I'm going to have to pay to keep us out of that hospital?'

'That's not his fault,' his sister said.

'How did they know where to find you and Lutek?' he asked me. 'They were there waiting, before you were. I saw them.'

I stood at the sink and rubbed my eyes with the back of my hand. I couldn't work out how to get the water going. 'Maybe they got lucky,' his sister said.

'They weren't even keeping watch,' he told her. 'And when I asked you where he was then, you said you didn't know,' he said to me.

He waited for me to answer.

'You just woke him up,' his sister said.

'Well?' he said.

'Sh'maya thinks only of himself,' I told him.

He looked at me. 'If it had been my turn to go with you, it would have been me,' he said.

His sister told him she didn't understand, so he explained it to her, I was an informer. I worked for the Gestapo. His sister backed up a step and looked at me like I had two heads.

'Won't he tell the Germans if you throw him out?' she asked.

'No,' he told her, looking at me.

I dressed on the street in the snow. People passing by didn't seem to find it strange. I pulled the sweater my mother had boiled over three of my shirts. My socks were soaked when I put on my shoes but they warmed up after a while.

There was nowhere to go. I spent the day walking around.

When curfew came I climbed down a covered cellarway and moved a rubbsh bin to block the wind but still got so cold I had to move.

I made it to Adina's building after hiding every few minutes because of the patrols. I knocked on her window and at first she wouldn't open the shade and then she wouldn't let me in. Finally, when I stood on the street and called her name, she opened the window a crack and tossed out some bread.

'Are you crazy?' she said. 'Do you want to get me killed too?'

'I'm sorry,' I told her.

'This is all I have,' she said about the bread and then told me not to come back again and sent me away sobbing and eating it.

Toward the end of the night I found the block where Boris had ambushed the kid from the other gang and crawled down under the rubble into the caved-in cellar. I felt around in the dark for a place I could lie down. The kid he'd hit with the brick was gone. I stayed there and stole from street vendors or smaller kids when I got too hungry. I was a thief that caretakers and porters chased away from their doorways with sweeps of their brooms. I drank snowmelt collected in a can. I lay for days under some blankets. When I went out for food starving people slipped out of dark corners and followed me and when one beggar got hold of something the rest of the pack knocked him down and ripped what he had from his hands and then others stole it from them. Once whatever it was was eaten, everyone went back to begging.

I tried to make myself invisible but kids who had nowhere to go were everywhere and the smaller ones trailed anyone who might have a better situation. I ran away from them but three or four found my cellar and told their friends.

After that I wandered without a plan. I was always without a plan. I slept between the chairs on an old orchestra stand.

It got colder. A woman on the street felt bad when she saw me and gave me an extra pair of stockings to go over my socks but the elastics were broken. I helped another woman carry a milk canister and when we got to her place she gave me an extra coat.

I stole some cooked potatoes and when I finally stopped running and thought I was safe I walked right into Lutek's sister.

'My God, how you look!' she said. She burst into tears and asked what had happened to her brother. She still had her stutter. She kicked at me and when a yellow policeman came over her friend dragged her away. I found myself on my hands and knees in the slush. The policeman stood over me and nudged me with his foot. Then he left. While I was weeping someone stole the potatoes I had taken.

It warmed up a little so my feet and hands got better. I lost track of the days. I passed a clinic that treated eye infections and started going inside. I let everyone in line get ahead of me so I could sit in the warm waiting room for a few hours. I found one of the buildings where they'd restarted a grammar school and slipped in and took a seat in the back. The teacher noticed but seemed to know why I was there and didn't throw me out. Then through the window I saw Lutek's father pass by outside and I never went back.

Near the hospital where my mother died I saw Lejkin and some other police stop someone and hid until they were gone.

I wandered the streets. I spent nights wedged into crannies like a spider. I gave up on thinking ahead. I walked back and forth.

A boy my age caught me trying to steal from his father's shop while he was watching it and knocked me down with a club he had behind the counter and while I sat there crying and rubbing my head he tied my wrists with a rope and then tied the rope to a cart he had outside. He hefted the cart's handles and started dragging me. I slipped and stumbled trying to free myself. He was talking about how tired he was of this and how he was going to take me to the Germans himself. But he tied the knot too loose and by scraping it against the back of the cart I got it free. He still didn't know, dragging his cart along, and the street he turned us onto was empty. I looked at the back of his head. Somewhere he had a mother hoping he'd come home safe. I could take him from her like my mother was taken from me. But instead when I passed an alley I dropped the rope and ran.

I couldn't even do that right, I thought later. I sat on the pavement with my back to the wall. People stepped over my legs.

At curfew someone lifted me off the pavement. I was dozing and shaking from the chill. I was carried many blocks and then down some steps to the basement of a bombed-out house. The room where I was laid down onto a bed was very bright and all around me was noise and confusion. There were bunk beds made from rough boards against the walls. The place was filled with kids on the floor and on the bunks and all of them were dirty and all of them were making noise, Some were playing cards and others were playing with knives. No one seemed to be supervising them.

I couldn't feel my feet. 'This one's in a bad way,' the man who'd been carrying me told someone else, and I recognized his voice. 'This is a satellite shelter,' he told me when he saw that I was awake. 'A place people can go who need to get off the streets for curfew. You can have a little soup and warm up and then tomorrow you can go home.'

'I don't have a home,' I told him, and Korczak looked at me like he'd already known that was what I was going to say.

'Well, then, we'll have to think about adding you to our little group,' he said. And the kids on the bunks made loud sounds of protest, to make it clear that was the last thing they needed.

The real orphanage was nicer than the shelter but the kids were the same. It was on Sienna Street facing the wall, as far south as you could go. One of the kids said they'd had to move again in October when the ghetto had got even smaller. Korczak and the heavy woman, Stefa, washed me. He said while they were doing it that he'd never seen such a dirty chest and armpits.

Everyone slept on the first floor in one big room and in the morning wooden chests and cupboards were dragged around, mostly by the heavy woman, to make areas where we could eat and study and play. She told the kids to help and some would and some wouldn't. All of this went on while I stayed in bed, watching. 'Who is he, the Prince?' another kid asked, and Korczak told him I was recovering from frostbite.

My feet were burning and while she was sliding a cupboard over near me the woman said I should set them in a pan of cold water, but she didn't make me so I didn't. I only got up for lunch and dinner and when I did it made my feet burn even more. Lunch was a wheat porridge ground up in a meat grinder and then steeped in boiling water and dinner was potato skins mushed into patties and pigweed with turnips. While the kids at my table ate they sang *Julek and Mańka went out of town and kissed so hard the trees fell down.*

'Who weeps at turnips?' a kid said when he saw what I was doing. But I was seeing Lutek still hanging onto his sack in the back of the blue policeman's car.

'My eyes do this,' I told everyone at the table. 'I don't know why.'

After lunch there'd been a class in Hebrew in a corner of the room near my bed. I pulled the covers over my face. Korczak asked questions in Polish and the kids answered in gibberish. Sometimes he corrected them. His last question was, 'Are you happy here in Palestine?' and it sounded like everyone had the right answer. The woman said it was time for chores and I could hear everyone getting to their feet and when I pulled the covers down kids were sweeping the floors and washing the walls and wiping the windows. Everyone was calling for something and banging around and knocking into things. When that was finished they all came back near my bed again, and Korczak said it was time to read his column in the orphanage newspaper. This week's column was called 'Take Care with the Machine.' 'The machine doesn't understand; the machine is indifferent,' he read. He had his glasses on the end of his nose and used his finger to follow the print. 'Put your finger in, it'll cut it off; put your head in, it'll cut that off too.' I got up to pee. My feet weren't burning so much.

The toilet was in the back behind the kitchen. There were eleven kids in line for it. 'Is this the only toilet?' I asked.

'This is the only toilet,' the kid ahead of me said without turning around.

Going back to bed I stopped at the window. It was bright outside. The sun had dried dead flies on the windowsills. The bricks under the sills moved like loose teeth where the mortar was gone. Magazine photographs tacked below were so speckled with holes they must have been targets for wall games.

The kid who'd been in front of me in line spent the rest of the afternoon sweeping the top step of the landing. I watched him. He kept his eyes on me while he worked. When he wasn't sweeping he waved a hand around his face like a horse shoos flies away with its tail.

He had the bed next to me and shook me awake for breakfast the next morning. We had hot water and saccharine and bread. You could eat three pieces if you wanted. We got in line to be weighed and measured afterwards. While I waited a cripple in front of me waved his stump at me like a fin.

I was back on my bed looking at my feet when the kid with the broom carried over a pan of water filled to the brim and spilled some of it setting it on the floor next to me.

'Madame Stefa says to soak your feet in this,' he said.

'What's floating in it?' I asked.

'How would I know?' he said.

I asked his name and he said Zygmuś. He said he'd banged his hand. While I soaked my feet he watched the blood swell along his fingernail and wiped it off on the floor, leaving red smears.

The heavy woman asked from across the room if there wasn't something he was supposed to be doing and he told her he was helping me.

He introduced me to the kid two beds over. The kid was Mietek from the Chłodna Street gate but he acted like he'd never seen me. Zygmuś said they were best friends but the kid didn't look up and just sat on his bed staring at his rotten boots.

I asked what was wrong with him and Zygmuś said the kid's mother had been sick

161

but had promised him she wouldn't die until he was safe in the orphanage. Then she died as soon as he got there.

'Pan Doctor says he's suffering from pangs of conscience,' Zygmuś' said. The kid didn't seem to hear.

The joke around the orphanage was that no one had ever seen the kid smile, Zygmuś said. The kid said without smiling, 'That's not true. I smile all the time.' Then he turned away from us.

'What's he holding on to?' I asked.

'That's his dead brother's prayer book,' Zygmuś said.

The heavy woman finally got him working and I sat there soaking my feet. I was happy I was warm and not on the street. Later Korczak stood over me and gestured at the pan and asked to take a look. He had this expression like he knew what needed to be done but was being prevented from doing it. His glasses had thumbprints on the lenses. A kid who was six or seven kicked down some girls' toy city in the play area and they all started yelling and crying.

'Is that Jerzyk?' the heavy woman asked him from across the room.

'That's Jerzyk,' he said to me like we were sharing a secret. He lifted my foot out of the pan and squeezed my toes. He said, 'For two years he's been making my life miserable. He made everyone miserable in kindergarten. I wrote an article about him that advocated penal colonies. And he's so young, yet! Imagine what'll happen when he's grown.'

Two of the older kids took Jerzyk by the arms and pulled him away from the girls. Korczak decided my feet had healed enough for me to work and told the heavy woman so and she came over and gave me the job of the chamber pots, which she said had to be rinsed with ammonia. She called it starting at the bottom. I asked why they needed chamber pots when they had a toilet and she said that one toilet served a hundred and fifty children and twenty staff members. She also said that if I was finished asking questions, then this might be a good time to start earning my keep.

★ ★ ★

After the lights were switched off that night and we were settled on our beds Korczak appeared out of the darkness and sat on mine. 'I saw you at the window this afternoon,' he said. He was being as quiet as he could. 'It's annoying to have to stand on tiptoe and barely see out, isn't it? Like not being able to see in a crowd.' I agreed with him. 'Tomorrow is Thursday and Thursday is when the admissions committee meets to review the new applicants,' he added. 'Has Madame Stefa talked to you about the application?' After I shook my head he asked, 'Can you write?'

'A little,' I told him.

'Do I intrude on your business?' he asked Zygmuś. Zygmuś rolled over on his bed.

'She'll help you with it tomorrow,' he told me. 'Do you have any family at all?'

I cleared my throat and had nowhere to spit so I swallowed it. 'You'll be fine,' he said, after he put a hand on my face and felt my tears.

My weeping seemed to tire him out. 'The whole thing's become just a formality anyway,' he said. 'Someone mentions the candidate, no one says anything, we all stare into space, and then after a few minutes someone else asks who it was we were talking about in the first place. Someone makes a motion to accept, someone else complains about lunch, and the discussions slide around like a drunk on an icy hill.'

A few other kids rolled over or made other noises. At the far end, one snored like a snuffling pig. 'Everyone starts out with big plans,' I told him. 'Then they figure out that's not how things are going to be.'

He laughed to himself. 'The Book of Aron, chapter 2, verse 2,' he said. 'And mostly what they achieve is weakened eyesight and tired feet.'

His ears looked even wider and his neck even thinner in the dark. I didn't know what he wanted. 'When I think about all the strength I squandered in just blundering around,' he said.

He asked if I did a good job on the chamber pots. I told him I did. He told me their condition would often let you know the quality of an orphanage.

He stayed where he was sitting. He seemed to be listening to everyone's breathing.

I asked if he remembered that boy he was carrying after the city surrendered. The one who needed the shoes.

'That boy,' he said. 'Of course. The morning the British entered the war we joined a crowd outside their embassy. Poles and Jews rubbing shoulders like brothers again! Everyone singing 'Poland Is Not Yet Lost!' That same afternoon seven shells hit the orphanage. One blew out the window-panes of the dining hall and another blew my hat off. I remember telling him we had to leave the street because my bald head was too clear a target for the planes.'

'Did he ever get his shoes?' I asked. But

even in the dark I could tell that he didn't want to talk about it.

'He used to go with me on my rounds,' he said. 'After the bombing we got a storekeeper to donate her lentils by arguing that the Germans would confiscate them anyway. I always remind those I'm asking that it's Jewish honor I'm upholding and they can either give to my orphans or the Germans. He was a lot like the boy who got into trouble today,' he said. 'Wherever a bruise or a bump on the head was involved, there he was.'

'Bad luck,' I said.

'There are people who just don't think,' he said, 'just like some don't smoke.'

I didn't answer. I wanted someone to miss me like that.

'But you couldn't get angry with him,' he said. 'It's like Slowacki said: God loves power the way he loves wild horses.'

He patted my leg like he thought I was the boy who was gone. 'A lot of people are afraid to sleep during the day because they worry it'll spoil their night,' he said. 'It's the reverse with me.'

I took his hand and he didn't move it away. Something about that made me start weeping again.

'Lately I've been smelling schmaltz at night,' he told me. 'Do you smell it?'

I shook my head.

'It drives me crazy,' he said.

'I don't smell it,' I said.

'I think about Europe in Polish,' he said. 'And I think about Palestine in Hebrew. But I think about eating in Yiddish.'

'I just think about eating,' I said. It made him chuckle again.

He told me the next day I should help with the coal delivery and I said I would. He started talking to himself about it. He said now you had to give the coal man twenty złotys extra to get whole pieces and not just chips. He said if the rumors about the Germans requisitioning even more were true, then we could all start burning furniture. Of course, he said, if you gave the Jews a single quiet day, each one of them would start producing rumors.

'Everyone wants to figure out what to do next,' I told him.

'We can't even see to the bottom of the cup we hold in our hands,' he said, then blew his nose into a handkerchief and wished me a good night.

'Good night,' Zygmuś said.

'My apologies for having disturbed you,' Korczak told him.

'What was that all about?' someone else said out of the darkness after he'd left.

'Pan Doctor isn't doing so well,' Zygmuś said. I could hear his yawn.

'What does that mean?' I asked.

'Go to sleep,' he answered.

* * *

I turned out to be good at unloading coal, which meant I was covered in coal dust from the waist down and not head to toe. I also helped with a shipment of groats that the heavy woman mixed with horse blood for our breakfast. I was invited to join the choir and told them I couldn't sing, and invited to join the drama club and said I couldn't act. The heavy woman talked to me about my application and seemed to think my situation was more than pathetic enough and I needn't worry about being kicked out onto the street. And she told me to please start calling her Madame Stefa.

The Germans told Korczak the window-panes now needed to be covered with black paper at night and so she sat me at a worktable and carried over a crate filled with paste and scissors and rolls of black paper and put me in charge of four other kids in making the shades. When they wouldn't listen to me she told Zygmuś to help out. He asked why it was his job but she only gestured to

168

where she wanted him to sit and then left. He gathered up his friend Mietek and two others and told them that it was the health officer's orders and when Mietek asked why he called her the health officer, Zygmuś said that the real health officer wouldn't speak to Jews but just pointed at the pots he wanted lifted in order to see whether the bottoms were clean.

He had me measure and the others do the cutting and pasting. The kids talked about nothing but eating. One said that when he was young he could go all day without eating but now he was an empty pot. He said that the soup was no sooner poured down into his stomach than he was hungry again. He had the same blank and accepting expression as my little brother and I had to stop looking at him. I moved a stepstool over to the windows and did arm lengths to estimate sizes.

One of the other kids asked Zygmuś if he had any brothers or sisters and he said he had three sisters. He said his parents used to have a mill that ground buckwheat flour and one day he and his sisters had gone to get milk and when they returned, people were robbing the mill and a neighbor was saying, 'You people are robbing these kids and they're orphans,' and that's how they found out their parents had been killed. He said his older sister had then been attacked by some

169

German soldiers and had run away over the Russian border and that really put them out of business as a family since she'd been the only one left who could cook.

Madame Stefa was in charge of the daily routine. Her scoldings always began with 'Let me tell you,' and when she was asked a question she didn't want to answer she always said, 'Let's not worry about it.'

Korczak spent two days a week arranging for help for other orphanages and the rest of the time he went begging for us. On those days he left early and returned late and always took a different boy. He begged at the Jewish Community Office and the homes of the rich or the collaborators and outside the cafés. The heavy woman worried about him. She said when he was gone that he came back in the evenings worn out from having had to raise hell over a barrel of sauerkraut.

Zygmuś said the kids he picked to go along were the ones who'd been with him since they were small, that he liked the kids he'd raised more than the rest.

I watched him late at night when he got back. With only one light on, he looked ancient. His hands shook and he rationed his cigarettes and vodka with saccharine and every few minutes he cleared his throat.

'So you're up again,' he said one night

when he finally saw me watching. 'Aren't you tired? Don't we give you enough to do?'

I was always tired, I told him. And whatever I had to do I couldn't handle.

'So you're not one of my fire-eaters?' he asked. 'Like your friend Zygmuś? Whose mother rode stags through the forest and ate horses?'

My mother took in washing, I told him.

'I remember you from the gang at the gate,' he said. And when I apologized he told me it was all right. I hadn't been the cruel one and everyone had to do what they needed to in order to get by. All doors opened before the hungry.

He shook me awake on my bed the next day and told me to get dressed because I was coming with him.

When we got outside it was still dark. I didn't want to be back out on the streets, I told him. He said he understood.

He talked nonstop as he walked. He said maybe today we'd visit the Germans. He said the officer assigned to supervise the orphanage had been a pediatrician himself and always referred to Korczak as his 'respected colleague' and thought that was hilarious. He said the officer called the orphanage his 'republic of swindlers' and said the Jews managed to adjust to every situation but never knew how good they had it, like the man who complained he had no golden shoes but didn't realize that he was soon to lose his legs.

It was windy and muddy and cold and everyone who was out early moved around as if fed up with his own exhaustion. Most were beggars who'd been out all night. We stopped next to a girl with bare arms squatting in front of a little wagon carrying frozen and rotted rutabagas, A younger girl was curled up under the wagon with her feet covered in newspaper wrapped and tied into the shape of shoes. Korczak knelt next to her and put something in her hand. Both girls did everything slowly.

'Enough about the Germans,' he said, once we started walking again. He blew on his hands. He talked about how some of the orphanage girls had surprised him with a movie they made with a waxed paper box and electric bulb.

I asked where we were going and he asked if it mattered. He said that given one circumstance or another we were all tied up like dogs on a chain.

After I didn't answer he apologized for saying something so unhelpful.

His apology made him quiet. In the darkness we passed Przejazd Street and the

Immortal Hole and the building with the slanted roof and the dormers.

He said that in one house the previous week he found six children on a wet and rotting mattress. And when I still didn't say anything he asked who *wasn't* sad? He said the world was one great sadness. He said what we needed to do was tell ourselves that we weren't living in the worst place in the world but instead were surrounded by grasshoppers and glowworms.

From his expression it didn't look like he was being ironic. I told him again that I didn't want to be out on the street and when he didn't answer I said I didn't want to be at the orphanage either. He said I was free to leave and I hated him for making me feel the way I did and hated myself even more for not just being dead somewhere.

The sun came up and he asked if I was at least happy to be out in the sunshine. I rubbed my arms and face and he asked if I'd heard him. I told him that whether I was happy or unhappy, I took things as I found them. He said his mother used to say when it was sunny and he was particularly gloomy that not even a Jew could suffer on a day like today.

Every few steps now someone was begging or selling or had come out of a hole and was trying to keep warm. One was wrapped in a quilt that was losing feathers in the wind. Someone was selling milk out of their house and we got in line for some. 'Wherever there's a line I stand in it, no matter what they're selling, because I know I'm going to get something,' he joked.

We began our begging at a rich man's house. He rang the bell. The man when he answered the door said, 'Oh, Pan Doctor, you're killing me here,' instead of hello, and Korczak asked him what was worse than being an old man and then answered being an old Jew. And what was worse than that? An old Jew who was penniless. And worse than that? An old Jew who was penniless and unresourceful. And worse than that, an old Jew who was penniless and unresourceful and who bore the burden of a large family. And worse than that, someone whose large family were all children. And worse than that, children who were starving.

The man disappeared from the door and returned with some money and dumped it into a sack Korczak held out. Then he excused himself and said good morning and shut the door while Korczak looked into the sack.

He led me to the next house. He said he himself had been well-to-do until his father

174

had to be put into a mental hospital. And that's when he learned what it meant to have to turn to adults for help. Adulthood was a privileged position against which he'd had to struggle. He'd heard a lot about the proletariat as a teenager, but the world's oldest proletariat was the child. The child was hounded even by those who loved him. He'd decided then and there that he'd become the father of orphans and would always work for those who should come first but always came last.

'Like you, I was always slow doing everything,' he said. 'When my grandmother would watch me at a chore she'd always say, 'You. Philosopher.''

'When my father called for my help he always said, 'Hey! Bungler!'' I told him.

'And you always helped him,' he said.

'I didn't like to work,' I told him.

'The laziest person I ever knew was a man named Krylov who spent the entirety of his adult years on his couch, with all of his books beneath it,' he said. 'He would just reach down and read whatever came to his hand.'

We walked to other houses and when the people who answered the door said no he wouldn't go away. He just repeated, 'But my children. My children.' I thought about my mother. 'Stay still while I'm talking,' he told me between houses.

At lunchtime we stood inside the door of a café and he shouted, 'Is there someone here who can get my children through the winter?' And a man called him over and he approached some others, thanking those who gave and saying about what went into the sack, 'Not enough, not enough.' In the afternoon we stopped at the post office to go through the packages that were undeliverable after the German soldiers had opened them.

Walking back to the orphanage we passed Mrs Melecówna's parlor. The pavement was blocked by kids standing with their hands out and weeping. He gave something to each.

After we'd gone a few blocks I asked if he wanted to rest because he looked so tired. He said we'd got to the point where dead children no longer impressed us. He said that if a man couldn't look on calmly at the death of another then his own life was worth a hundred times more. He was having enough trouble walking that he leaned on each house railing we passed. He said it was like how some people still went to visit relatives who'd been taken to the hospital.

A pack of kids ran by us and almost knocked him down. He half-sat against a post. His breathing sounded like my mother's and I thought I would have to run away and leave him on the street if he kept making those sounds. He said to himself that the smugglers lived a little longer and the unenterprising died in silence.

Then he didn't speak again until we turned onto Sienna and could see the orphanage. I thought if he died on the street, where would I be then? He took my hand to stop me and looked at where we were going like the building itself could kill him.

Jerzyk and some other boy were playing in the street with some rope, taking turns whipping each other. We could hear their laughter, 'You know what I dream of?' Korczak said. 'A room in Jerusalem with a table and something to write on. Transparent walls so I wouldn't miss a single sunrise or sunset. And I'm just the silent Jew from who knows where.'

We stood where he'd stopped us. He held the lamppost to keep himself steady. Then he made an after-you gesture with a bow and cleared his throat behind me all the way down the street.

★ ★ ★

'Did you think you were going to hide in that orphanage until the war was over?' Lejkin asked. I hadn't realized he was behind me on

177

the street. I'd been sent out with Zygmuś and a handcart to pick up a barrel of pickles someone had told Korczak he'd donate.

'Let's have a talk,' Lejkin said. 'Your friend can handle the stolen goods.'

I stopped and Zygmuś kept pulling. He rattled the cart over the tram tracks and around the corner and out of sight.

'They're not stolen,' I said.

'Our friend Obersturmführer Witossek thought I should remind you that you're still a member of the anti-crime unit,' Lejkin said. 'It's not as though our problems have gone away while you've been settling in at your new home.'

I shoved him as hard as I could. 'You said they weren't hunting smugglers,' I said.

He straightened his collar and stuck out his chin. 'The Germans do what the Germans do,' he said. 'What *you* want to remember is how to keep them from doing it to you.'

He said I should let him buy me a hot chocolate and pulled me to a café down the street.

The café was full and warm enough from its stove that its windows ran with condensation. Outside of it a boy sat cross-legged with a baby next to him on a spread handkerchief, the baby on its side and panting like a pigeon. Inside we sat there looking at each other and he handed me a napkin for my eyes. 'You cry more than any other person I know,' he said. A woman approached our table and he said, 'Watch: this one carries a photograph of herself from happier days to show what a wreck she's become.'

When the waiter came he ordered for me. He asked if I'd heard about Lübeck and when I said no he told me, after making certain no Germans were near, that the British had bombed it flat. When I didn't say anything he said that everyone in the Order Service, optimists and pessimists alike, believed Germany would lose in the end, but the pessimists claimed that before that happened Germany would gain control of the world. The optimists said Germany had waged total war in Poland, lightning war in France, an instalment war in England, and a fatal war in Russia. He said people had started writing 1812, the year of Napoleon's defeat, on the walls.

He said he'd asked Witossek when he thought the war would end and Witossek had answered when Germans were eating once a day and Jews once a month.

When the hot chocolates arrived he toasted to good fortune and when I asked what good fortune he said he was moving up in the Order Service and was now Szeryński's deputy. So you could say he was second in command of the entire yellow police.

He was just making conversation, he said finally, when I still hadn't answered.

I told him I needed to get back.

He said they would like me to tour certain areas with them in case I might have some hard-won knowledge that would come in handy.

'You want me to help you kill someone else?' I said.

He asked if I wanted my hot chocolate and when I didn't answer he drank it. 'The requisitioning is about to get more extreme,' he said. 'No potatoes. No bread. No coal for the orphanages but plenty for the coffee-houses.'

What could any of us do, I told him. None of us had any luck.

'Think of it like this,' he said. 'Are we to dole out spoonfuls to everyone, with the result that no one will survive? Or give a fuller measure to the few?'

'I need to get back,' I said.

'I'm going to talk to you as though you can understand,' he said. 'Shyster to shyster, as it were. Those with no talent for swindling always suffer.' He gestured outside. 'You and I both know that no compassion can be expected from the Germans. Whether we live or die depends on how long they're in power. If they have enough time, they'll kill us all. If not, some can be saved.'

I stood up and he didn't try to stop me. 'We won't need you until the end of the week,' he said.

'Why do you need *me*?' I said. 'Why can't you get someone else?'

He ran his finger around the inside of my cup. 'It'll help to think about others the way my boss Szeryński does,' he said, then stood up himself and made an after-you gesture like Korczak's. 'He says that refugees are like autumn leaves.'

He followed me out onto the street. It had begun to snow and he pulled up his collar and then pulled up mine. Then he cleaned off his seat and got on his bicycle and rode away. Because of the snow it slipped and slid all over on the cobblestones and he had to put his foot out every so often for balance.

★　★　★

The other staff members slept in a building next door but Korczak had his office and bed on the floor above us in what everyone called the isolation ward for the kids who were the sickest. His bed and night table were in the middle of the room with the kids' beds arranged around them. Each bed had a pail next to it on the floor and all the kids had compresses on their heads. Korczak looked to be asleep, even though his lamp was lit and his clothes were still on. The kids were asleep. It was after four in the morning.

There was a heel of black bread on the table and another piece in his hand, as if he'd fallen asleep eating.

I had crept up the stairs to talk to him. I heard a noise and hid behind his desk and then Madame Stefa appeared in the doorway and watched him sleep before moving over to the side of his bed.

'I always try to nap for an hour before the beehive starts to buzz,' he told her, and I realized he was awake though his eyes were still closed. 'When I was a child, I pretended to be asleep and then opened my eyes suddenly so I could see my guardian angel before he could hide.'

She lowered herself to sit on the edge of one of the kids' beds. She looked as tired as he did. 'How was your day today?' she asked. 'We didn't get a chance to talk.' And I could hear in her voice what I'd heard in my mother's when she'd asked me for news.

'Ten hours and seven calls,' he said. 'Fifty złotys and another promise of five a month.'

She said no one expected him to spend ten

hours tramping around in the cold and that his ailments were not going to allow it.

'Which ailments are those?' he asked. He was still on his back but his hand was now over his eyes.

'Your weakened heart muscle. Your pleurisy from pneumonia. Your bladder trouble. Your swollen legs and feet,' she said. 'Your hernia.'

They were quiet. 'It's not funny,' she said.

'How did the doctor who refused to perform the hernia operation put it?' he asked. 'My health is in ruins.'

Go downstairs, I thought to myself. I needed to talk to someone about Lejkin. But what would I say?

'You cough and you complain and then you go out without your sweater,' Madame Stefa said.

'What about you? One can't give you anything,' Korczak said.

He lifted his hand from his eyes and saw her looking at the vodka and water on the table, 'Have you noticed that bread and water taste better at night?' he asked.

'And what happens when someone takes you off the street?' she asked. 'Where will we be then?'

Her anger made him angry too. 'Who says that when I go out the Germans will be about?' he said. 'And if they are, who says they'll be on my street? And if they are, who says they'll choose me? And if they do, who says they won't be persuaded by what I have to tell them?'

'I'm just asking if it's worth the risk for such a little bit of money,' she said.

He made a noise with his mouth. Then he said, 'You know, when I was a child I told my teachers that I knew how to remake the world. Throw away all the money was always step one. My plan always broke down at step two.'

She closed her shawl around her neck with one hand. It was cold. The caretaker's son called up from the courtyard to complain about the light. He said it looked like Hanukkah and he didn't want to have to tell them again. Madame Stefa went to the windowsill and refastened the blackout paper.

'I have a recurring dream in which one of my boys says about me, 'He went to sleep when we needed him most,'' Korczak said.

'You can't do everything,' she said.

'How much land have I tilled?' he said. 'How much bread have I baked? How many trees have I planted? How many bricks have I laid? How many buttons have I sewn, how many garments have I patched?'

'Sssh,' she told him. 'Don't work yourself up.'

'My father called me a clod and an idiot and a crybaby and an ass,' he said. 'He was right. And so were those who believed in me.'

I realized they were talking about something else completely and that I didn't know how anyone's mind worked, including my own.

'I know you never promised me anything,' she said. 'And I lie awake telling myself, Stefa, you old fool, you got what you deserved.'

'The most splendid assumption still needs verification,' he told her.

'I just always believed that one receives in order to nourish,' she said.

'So what is love?' he asked. 'Is it always given to those who deserve it? How do we know if we love enough? How do we learn to love more?'

The room smelled of cigarettes and feet. The blackout paper came loose again and outside the window it was starting to get light.

'Did you ever love anyone?' she asked.

'From seven to fourteen I was permanently in love,' he said, 'and always with a different girl.'

The windowpanes rattled and it looked like he was listening to the wind. He gave a big sigh.

'I always think that maybe if I hadn't been so ugly,' she said.

'I tell everyone, 'Stefa always reminds me that I'm a miserable human being who makes everyone else miserable,'' he said.

She said something so quietly as an answer that he asked her to repeat it. 'It's just hard always feeling alone,' she said.

He didn't answer so she looked at her hands. My legs cramped from having been in one position for so long.

'I've got back what I paid in,' he finally told her, 'Loneliness isn't the worst thing. I value memories.'

She stood up and crossed to the door and stopped. 'I remind myself that it's not my place to ask for things,' she said. 'But even now my ego gets in the way.'

Even I could see her unhappiness in the lamplight, but he ignored it. 'Nothing I can say or do can spare you or spare myself,' he said.

'Always you give up, you postpone, you cancel, you substitute,' she told him.

He sat up on his elbows. 'I see my feelings through a telescope,' he said. 'They're a little gang huddled on a polar plain. When someone coughs, first I feel pity and then its opposite: maybe he's contagious. Maybe he's going to cause us to use up the rest of our medicine.'

She said she was sorry and that she'd let him sleep.

'I exist not to be loved but to act,' he told her.

'The saint orders and God executes,' she said.

'I'm doing what I can,' he said. 'Our God may not have the will to enforce the Law, but that doesn't mean we shouldn't obey it.'

'Whom do we sue for breach of contract?' she asked.

'Rabbi Yitzchak of Berdichov is supposed to have summoned God to a rabbinic court,' he told her.

'I suppose we were never going to find a place where we'd enjoy perfect digestion and eternal peace,' she said.

'Sometimes I think: don't fall asleep,' he said. 'Just listen for another ten minutes to their breathing. Their coughing. Their little noises.'

'Yes,' she said. 'That's what I do.'

'We're living tombstones,' he told her. 'Israel is where they have the baby carriages and the green growing things.'

She made a noise like he'd slapped her and he fell back onto his bed once he heard her going down the stairs.

A boy everyone called Mandolin because he never let go of his instrument, even holding it above his head during his lice bath, died in his bed with both arms wrapped around it. We were eating less at meals and everyone was frantic about it. If we finished our portions too soon we had a longer wait until the next meal and our torture grew. All anyone could think about was the table's next loaf of bread. In the isolation ward when the soup kettle went round a forest of little hands rose from the beds. We had soupy oat flour cooked in water and horse blood curdled in pieces and fried in a pan. It looked like scraps of black sponge and tasted like sand. On the Sabbath a broth of buckwheat and lard.

Though there was no food, Korczak had us all address and mail invitations to our Passover Seder on April first. We divided up his list of benefactors. When the day came, fifty guests arrived and sat near the door. The long tables were covered with tablecloths. I sat next to a kid whose blisters and scabs were so thick his neighbors called him Fish Scales. We had no eggs or bitter herbs and only a bit of soup and a matzoh ball each, and the smaller kids were excited because it was announced that Madame Stefa had hidden an almond in one of the matzoh balls, Our holiday starvation, Zygmuś joked, would be like the rest of our week. But Korczak told the guests that no child at his table had been abandoned and all were joined by the loving spirits of their absent mothers and fathers, and when he said that many of the kids started crying. Most of the audience did too. Mietek got the almond.

For a week no one came round to bother me. Then someone pounded on the orphanage door late in the evening, and Madame Stefa answered it and came over to my bed and said a Jewish policeman wished to see me.

At the door Lejkin said that he needed to find the apartment where my friend, the pretty one, had stayed before she'd left the ghetto. I said I didn't know what he was talking about and he said if I refused then the Germans he was with would take ten kids from the orphanage and shoot them. He said the Germans would be happy to tell me which ones they would shoot. He waited while I got dressed and then walked me down the stairs and we got into a car with Germans in the back. One of them asked him in Polish why I was crying and Lejkin said, 'That's what he does.'

At first I gave them the wrong address but

once we stopped there I panicked and told them I'd been mistaken and gave them the right one. That was only seven blocks farther on. Something was caught in the heater in the car's dashboard and made a fluttering sound. While I waited in the front seat, Lejkin and two Germans went up to the door and knocked and asked the woman who answered to step outside. She was in her red flowered bathrobe. She looked over at me in the car. One of the Germans shot her where she stood and they left her there outside her front door.

The next day the kids were talking about how many people had been shot all over the ghetto. Korczak told Madame Stefa to let me sleep, so the room was set up for the day around me. I told myself I wasn't going to move and if I cried until I dried out that was fine too. No one knew how many people had been killed. One of the staff members finally told Mietek that she'd heard they'd all been connected to an illegal newspaper, Korczak said this didn't need to be discussed with the children within earshot. The next day I was made to get up and do some chores and when I was washing dishes I overheard him tell Madame Stefa the Jewish Council had circulated a memorandum saying that the Germans said the executions had been a singular event and wouldn't be repeated.

After that there were daily roundups at barricades the Germans set up on different streets with a few sawhorses and signs. Once the barricades went up you only had a few minutes to get away before the cross streets and alleys were blocked too. 'Now the day's a success if you just manage to get where you're going without an incident,' Madame Stefa said.

Korczak's solution to all of this was letter-writing. Just because things were as bad as they could be, he said, that didn't mean we had to accept that action was useless.

All of those with acceptable penmanship were set to writing *Please if possible send packages to the Orphans' Home at 16 Sienna Street for the sick children.* He said there was more and that he would dictate the rest. He said to write that peaceably they run around and play, these children who so recently arrived wounded, frozen, abused, hungry, and hunted. Some of the kids asked how to spell peaceably and he told them it didn't matter. He said to write that there was no food for them and a lot of the smaller children had stopped growing. That nightmares and weeping were their permanent experiences. And yet his teaching had been borne out, since when the adult community wouldn't provide a stable or rational environment the children could create for themselves a world that was functional and tender. I wrote that sentence twice, I was so taken with it. He said to write that there were always more children imploring him to be admitted, coming to him in groups on the street and making their proposals like little skeletal aldermen. He said to sign the letters with our names and then *for Dr Henryk Goldszmit/Janusz Korczak/The Old Doctor from the Radio.*

★ ★ ★

For three days I didn't leave my bed except for meals, and Korczak again told them to leave me alone. The bedbugs spared only the bottom of my feet. During the day, before the kids hung the blackout paper, a new rule said they had to stand to the side of the windows to watch the street, because now the Germans were firing at any movement indoors. A policeman the staff members called Frankenstein because he looked and acted like the monster in the film never missed an opportunity, they said, to break a window if he saw a silhouette.

The kids watched the roundups at the barricades. They could hear them starting

192

with the whistles and the shouting. Sometimes they saw someone they knew. Jews went by carrying all sorts of things: cages or bowls or horns. One had a pot with a seedling in it. They were all going to the depot the Germans called the Umschlagplatz where the trains took them away.

On the fourth day Korczak again got me up to go on his rounds with him. Madame Stefa insisted he wear a warmer shirt and he had to struggle into it. She had to help him with his braces.

Out on the street he couldn't remember where he was going. In one doorway he rang the bell and said to me, 'What did I come to see him about?' In the gloom of another he said, 'What is it I'm looking at?' The instep of his shoe came loose and flapped when he walked. The coal smoke in the air left grit on our teeth. Everyone moved as if in a daze and looked at me like I was a piece of bread. A woman ahead of us in a shop complained about the price and Korczak said to her, 'Listen. These aren't goods and this isn't a store. You're not a customer and he's not a shopkeeper. So you're not being cheated and he's not profiting. This is just what we've decided to do, given that we have to do something.' On the way back his legs were so swollen he had to hire one of the bicycles with seats attached for passengers. He asked me to choose the strongest-looking driver and while we rode he leaned over to me and said in a hoarse voice that he was always moved by how gentle and quiet the drivers were, like oxen or horses.

★ ★ ★

More kids got sick but Madame Stefa still slept downstairs with the healthy ones and Korczak upstairs in the isolation ward. 'It's cold for May,' he said to me one night when I came up to sit with him. He was writing something while everyone else slept.

'What's that smell?' I asked.

'The carbide in the lamp,' he said.

The vodka bottle was gone. 'What's that?' I asked.

'Raw alcohol I mix with water and a dissolved hard candy for sweetener,' he said. He asked why I hadn't eaten dinner and when I told him I hadn't wanted to, he said fatigue and apathy were symptoms of malnutrition. I asked why he hadn't eaten dinner and he said eating was work and that he was tired.

I sat next to him on Jerzyk's bed. Jerzyk was sweating and his eyes were open. 'Alcohol mixed with warm water takes away the ache and sore eyes,' Korczak said.

While he wrote he kept his face close to the paper. 'What are you writing?' I finally asked.

He said it was to the Judenrat, requesting he be allowed to take over the public shelter that housed a thousand children on Dzielna Street. He said on his application he was spreading rumors that he was a thief who would let children starve so he could qualify for the job. He'd said he was unbalanced and excitable and his health had passed the test in the Gestapo's prison the year before: that despite the exacting conditions there, not once had he reported sick, not once had he requested a doctor, not once had he absented himself from work in the prison yard. He said he told them that he presently ate like a horse and slept soundly after ten shots of vodka and that experience had now endowed him with the ability to collaborate with criminals and born imbeciles.

'What does the job pay?' I asked him.

He said he'd requested a trial period and a minimum of twenty thousand złotys for the children's upkeep.

'Do you think you'll get it?' I asked.

'I already got it,' he said. 'I was handed the job permanently and given one thousand złotys. Who's going to deny the Old Doctor from the Radio the privilege of overseeing kids who are dying at the rate of ten a day?'

'So then what are you writing?' I asked him.

'I had imagined the criminal types among the personnel there would voluntarily leave since they obviously found the place so hateful,' he said. 'And they were bound to it only by cowardice and inertia. But instead they closed ranks against me. I'm the stranger. The enemy. The one good nurse died of tuberculosis. I'm trying to get the rest sacked.'

'The salt of the earth dissolves and the shit remains,' I told him. It was something Lutek always said.

'That describes it,' Korczak said.

Jerzyk told us he was thirsty and Korczak pulled himself off his bed and went down to the kitchen and returned with a cup of water. 'Here I have four ways of dealing with undesirable newcomers,' he said to me. 'I bribe them; I agree to anything; I lie low and mark time, waiting for the moment to strike; or I wear them out. There, none of these will work.'

'Thank you,' Jerzyk said, and Korczak told him he was welcome.

'Today everyone will be restless because I've got a headache,' he said. 'Or because it's cold. Or because they want an outing.' Jerzyk drank his water.

'Oh, listen to me,' he finally said, and put his hand on Jerzyk's head. 'I remember an old teacher who got indignant with us because our hair grew too fast.'

★ ★ ★

The next day he was too weak to go on his rounds but the day after I heard him exclaiming, 'I'm up! I'm up! I'm on my feet!' even from the floor below where I was sleeping.

'This one again?' Zygmuś said when he saw us getting ready to leave. 'I think Pan Doctor has a new favorite.'

We went to a butcher's shop Korczak had heard would be open for the day. 'Is this made from people?' he joked when the woman told him the price. 'It's too cheap for horsemeat.'

'How would I know?' she said. 'I wasn't there when they made it.'

On Twarda the road was blocked by Lejkin and a line of yellow police. He called to us and left his spot in the front to come over to talk.

'I understand you've been given new responsibilities,' Korczak told him. Lejkin bowed, and Korczak turned to me. 'Mr Szeryński was arrested for black marketing in furs.' I told him I didn't care and he explained that it meant my friend was now in command of the Order Service. I said he wasn't my friend and Lejkin said, speaking of that, one of the new imperatives was a daily quota for deportation and Service members who failed to fill their quotas would be departing themselves. And some of his men would prefer not to select their neighbors and maybe they could use the rest of my old gang since smugglers were always a good place to start.

'Leave the boy alone,' Korczak told him.

'I'm giving him fair warning,' Lejkin said. 'About business we'll be transacting in the future.' Korczak pulled me away.

'You needn't hide behind him,' Lejkin called. 'I can see you.'

But then he left us alone and Korczak told me after a few days that I could stop hiding. 'Mr Lejkin has other things to worry about,' he said.

It got hot again on Shavuot, the Feast of First Fruits, and the fly problem got so bad that Korczak finally set up a toilet-fee scale: you had to kill five flies to piss and fifteen to shit. Whoever was next in line was the one who checked. Mietek asked me one morning if he could kill them later because he couldn't hold it and I told him I'd do it for him.

Then at the beginning of June everyone had diarrhea and the chamber pots boiled over. Korczak and Madame Stefa figured it was something that had been in the bread. The Children's Home was now a home for the aged, he told her one night, and the whole group was worn down and mutinous and resentful. You could hear kids moaning on the chamber pots and on the toilet.

She said maybe the Germans would stop and he told her the Germans were running the world's largest enterprise and its name was war and they weren't playing at it and it wasn't clean or pleasant or sweet-smelling. He said that *We are the Germans* meant *We are the steel roller*. And then when she started to cry he said without sounding sorry that this was how he felt as well.

★　★　★

The night the yellow police came for me I was able to hide. There was shooting all night and Madame Stefa was weeping the next morning and wouldn't stop until Korczak had two of the staff members take her upstairs. He gathered the kids around him and told them that Madame was distraught because one of her favorite boys had been killed. He named the boy and no one knew him and he explained that he'd already graduated. One kid asked what was happening and he said no one knew but that night I overheard him tell Madame Stefa the Germans were exterminating all of the smugglers. Soldiers with dogs broke down doors and dragged people out of houses. The Order Service now patrolled the ghetto wall, They'd painted white numbers every fifty metres, with every policeman responsible for his own numbered area, The plan was apparently to use those Jews to starve all the other ones to death.

Madame Stefa remembered when the boy who'd been killed had helped bring in half a cow in six valises over the roof of a building that had been emptied by typhus, and how much the beef had thrilled all the children. She remembered that after the city surrendered he broke into a warehouse of army stores and came away with two pillowcases filled with rice and sugar.

She asked Korczak if he wanted tea, and he told her that if she wanted to make tea she should make some for Jerzyk, whose fever was worse. She asked if he wanted saccharine water and he said that if she wanted to make some saccharine water she should make it for a staff member who'd given his portion at dinner to one of the weeping little girls.

The next morning I was assigned the coal chute in the cellar and while I was down there Zygmuś came down the stairs with a carbide lamp. The carbide hissed. He said first that I looked like a chimney sweep and second that a boy had come to the door with a message for me and said that I'd know who he was. The boy said to tell me that Adina had come out of hiding because the Germans had called to her and told her they would kill her friends if she didn't. And that once she did, the Germans hung her in her apartment in front of her mother. And the boy wanted me to know he was going to find me and kill me. When he finished, Zygmuś made a face as if to say that was that, then kicked at some loose coal and took his lamp back up the stairs.

*　*　*

'You know about my other late-night companion, I assume,' Korczak told Madame Stefa when she appeared in his doorway and saw me sitting on Mietek's bed. Mietek had the fever now as well.

'You can't sleep?' she asked, and gave me a sympathetic look. The whole house was quiet.

Only a few kids were having noisy trouble breathing.

'There was so much wind and dust yesterday,' Korczak said, once she sat at the foot of Jerzyk's bed.

'For a while I thought the storm had cleared the air and it would make breathing easier,' she told him. It was so hot that kids had pitched their sheets onto the floor. Everyone who could walk had spent two days washing and washing the floor and it still smelled everywhere of the diarrhea.

I was with him because now each time the lights went out I remembered my mother when she woke and couldn't find me in the hospital and then her surprise at her inability to make a fist. I saw Lutek's face when his rabbit-skin cap flew off.

'While I was lying here I invented a machine,' Korczak said from on his back. 'It was like a microscope that could look into you. It had a scale that ran from one to a hundred and if I set the micrometer screw for ninety-nine, then everyone who hadn't hung on to at least one percent of his humanity would die. And when I ran the machine the only people left were mostly beasts. Everyone else had perished.'

'You've had a hard week,' Madame Stefa said.

'And after I set the screw to ninety-eight I was gone too,' he said.

'Yes, well, that would be terrible,' she said, and he let it go. Mietek flailed his arms in his sleep.

'The children now say even birds won't fly over us,' Korczak said, and she rubbed her face, tired or impatient. He said reading had begun to fail him and that this was a very dangerous sign.

'I saw Bula yesterday,' she told him. He smiled at the name and she went on. 'Can you imagine he's forty now? Not long ago he was ten. He asked me in for cabbage soup. He's still smuggling. He said each morning he gives his boy a half a pint of milk and a roll. I asked why he never visited and he said when he was well off there was never time and when he wasn't how could he come by looking so ragged and dirty?'

'Bula,' Korczak said, and they were quiet.

'Did you tell him that now he has to stop?' he finally asked.

'You know Bula,' she said.

'Do I have to do everything?' he said. 'Do I have to go and find him?'

'He's not going to listen,' she told him. And he closed his eyes and didn't answer.

'I have no idea what we're going to do with Balbina,' he told her instead. 'If you want to measure your resistance to going crazy, try helping a shlemiel.'

'She's still getting her bearings,' she said. 'She didn't have as much responsibility at the other orphanage.'

'You put the paper in her hand. She has to deliver it today; here is the address and the hour,' he said. 'But she's lost the paper or forgotten to take it with her or got frightened or the porter told her to go somewhere else. She'll go tomorrow. She'll go the next day. She'll go when she finishes the cleaning. And was it so important anyway?' He put his hand over his eyes and Madame Stefa told him that he was being unkind.

'I am unkind,' he said. 'To work here you have to be unkind. You have to be smeared with crap, you have to stink, you have to be crafty.'

'You seem presentable enough when you make your calls,' she said.

'I don't make calls,' he said; 'I go to beg for money and food. It's hard and degrading.'

'I know that,' she said.

'You,' he said to me. 'You never read. Do you want to sink into idiocy?'

'Leave him alone,' Madame Stefa said. 'He's making progress in his schooling.'

'His *schooling*?' he said. 'This is a prison. A plague ship. An asylum. A casino. A sprung trap. Bodies you clear from the street in the morning have piled up again by the evening.'

'That's no reason to frighten children,' she told him.

'Everyone's been tainted by this,' he said.

'You have a lot to do tomorrow,' she told him. 'You need to rest.' She filled his glass from the pitcher beside it. He took it and had a long swallow.

'Do you know how Jerzyk got here?' he asked. She took a deep breath and told him no. He said Jerzyk's whole family had died in quarantine and he'd dug up his father's body to get a golden dental bridge to sell for food but then had to use the money to buy his way out of the Umschlagplatz. 'Do you understand what I mean?' he said. 'He had to dig his father's head out of the dirt and then pull the bridge out of his father's mouth. And then he didn't get the food he needed anyway.'

Someone cried out downstairs and Madame Stefa left to investigate. Korczak was so still afterwards that I thought he'd fallen asleep.

He didn't open his eyes when she came back. 'I always think that the relief we feel after the roundups tells us something,' she said. 'Why are we relieved to be left *here*? And why are they starting with old people and children? Why would you begin by resettling those who'd have the most trouble in a strange place?'

Korczak sat up and poured himself another glass from the pitcher. Then he lay back down and closed his eyes without drinking it.

Dora had been rounded up twice and made it back each time, Madame Stefa told him. Dora said if they were ever taken to the Umschlagplatz to hang behind at the tail end of the march because when the trains got filled up they sometimes let the other people go.

Korczak said that was good advice.

'We shouldn't be speaking like this in front of the boy,' she said tiredly. Korczak agreed.

'Are you ever going to go to bed?' he asked me. I shook my head.

He seemed unsurprised. He said Korczak the dreamer was already far away. Outside of the city. Already in a desert and walking all by himself. He sees an unfamiliar country, he said. He sees a river and a bridge. He sees boats. And over there: small houses, cows and horses. He hadn't realized everything in Palestine was so small. He keeps walking, he said, until he can't walk anymore. He keeps walking, until the moment before he just falls down.

The next night Madame Stefa was too exhausted to stay awake so it was just the two of us. Then I fell asleep on Mietek's bed and when I woke it was almost light and Madame Stefa was getting the day's report. Korczak pulled the paper from one window but otherwise let everyone sleep. He told her Reginka had the rheumatic rash and that during the night he had administered salicylate until she'd heard ringing in her ears and seen yellow. She'd vomited twice and the lumps on her legs were turning pale and no longer hurt. He said Mietek was still having trouble breathing.

'Your cigarettes are probably not helping,' Madame Stefa said.

He told her that smoke was a good expectorant for the children and she answered that this was his theory. She said that sometimes when she came up to see him the air was so bad that *she* couldn't breathe. He said she reminded him of that entire stern regiment of women — wife, granny, cook — to which his father had always given in for the sake of peace.

'Is he asleep?' she asked, and I didn't hear his response but I didn't move. My head was turned away.

She said two of the girls no longer claimed to be hungry and seemed to be hibernating, Others were no longer sleeping because of hunger insomnia. She kept them covered but they were always thirsty and cold. Their stools were semi-liquid and muddled. When she pressed their skin the dimples lasted nearly two minutes. One was so clumsy with weakness she couldn't fasten a button. The hungriest were always appearing and disappearing around the kitchen. They all had scabies and crusted ringworm.

Death by famine lacked drama, Korczak told her. It was slow and dispiriting. At least until the crows or the rats or the dogs came along.

'Oh, stop it,' she told him.

'Am I being heartless?' he asked her.

'You're being unhelpful,' she told him.

'I find it helps if I tell myself that children can die or recover here,' he said, 'just as they do in a hospital.'

'Yes,' she said. 'Something strange happened today. When I emptied the chamber pots this morning I found a street boy outside our door.'

'I can smell the ammonia,' he said. 'And

that's not strange. Did you let him in?'

'He didn't want to come in,' she told him. 'He wanted to see into the main hall. I even stepped aside so he could look all he wanted. When I asked him his business he went on his way.'

'I know how he feels,' Korczak said.

I stayed by the window and watched the street that day and the next but saw no sign of Boris. One kid in a blue cap watched the orphanage both days but it wasn't him. I didn't go outside. Everyone claimed I was selfish because I took too long on the toilet. Everyone argued over who had had the worst night. Everyone was preoccupied with his morning temperature. 'What is it?' kids asked staff members who were still trying to read their thermometers. 'What was yours?' they asked one another.

At dinner Korczak announced the orphanage would be putting on a play called *The Post Office* by an Indian poet. It would be mounted on the third floor in the former ballroom, which would need to be cleaned and cleared for the event. The text was available to read for the next day or two and auditions would be held after that. One of the staff members, Esterka, would direct it. He asked her to stand to receive our thanks and she gave a wave.

There was a new girl whose brother had left her at the orphanage who kept everyone up with her nightmares and her crying. Her name was Gieńa and she was nine and during the day she didn't bother anyone though she didn't work either. Her father had died of tuberculosis and her mother and older sisters of typhus and before dropping her off her older brother had dressed her in so many ribbons and beads and colored crepe streamers that I made her laugh by asking if she was a Hottentot. She ate shielding her plate with her hand. In the dark she screamed so much that for a few nights since I was awake anyway I took her up to the third floor so everyone else could sleep. I sat with her while she wailed and she told me about her brother Samuel, who was seventeen and worked in one of the shops, and showed me how she stood on his feet and put her arms around his waist and was carried around the room when he marched. Her aunt had been unhappy because she said Gieńa ate all the bread and in no time it would all be gone and she told Samuel to put his sister in the orphanage so she didn't have to live with someone who was stealing from her. Telling her story calmed Gieńa down but the spiders on the third floor upset her. I said she could only go back down if she stopped screaming, so she promised she would and the next night when I checked she was awake and weeping but doing it quietly. She showed me a shell in her palm and chanted, 'Snail, snail, show me your horns,' and after we both watched for a minute it did.

★　★　★

Of course there wasn't enough for even the make-shift sets and costumes that Esterka had planned, Korczak told me early the next morning, standing over my bed, so it was time for Don Quixote and Sancho Panza to go back out on their rounds. I told him I didn't know what he was talking about and he said he was used to that. When I told him I didn't want to go he said he was used to that too.

'Can't someone else go?' I asked him. I was afraid of Boris.

'Madame Wilczyńska asked recently why I was so taken with you,' he said, while he waited for me to find my shoes. 'I don't see what's so puzzling about it.'

There was a boy out there who wanted to kill me, I told him. I didn't look at him when I spoke.

'You'll be fine with me,' he said. At the front door he stopped outside and pretended to check his pockets until I got the courage to follow. He told me I'd be awarded a Good Care Card for looking after one of the new arrivals. The card could be exchanged for an extra portion of sweets.

Again the only ones out that early were the beggars. Some were still in their nooks with their rubbish and others were wrapped in their odds and ends and crossing from person to person and begging. A boy who looked like my older brother had printed on his armband *Jew Useful for the Economy.* When he caught my eye he bared black teeth at me. 'And how are you?' he said. 'What time is left on *your* clock?' He kept his horrible expression even when Korczak gave him a few groszy. An elderly couple went around the three of us with their eyes on the pavement as if looking for something they'd lost.

The first house we tried gave Korczak all the money he needed after he described the play and then had a coughing fit. 'Well, that's good news,' he said, but once we started back two bodies in the street covered with sheets of paper made him stop. Where the papers weren't weighed down with stones they lifted in the wind.

We passed a mantelpiece clock wrapped with rope. 'You know, when I was a medical student I used to sit at night in the postmortem room after hours,' he said, after we started walking again. 'I paid the guard to let me stay there.'

I was scratching at lice. Even at the end my mother begged me to use the kerosene every day. Even at the end I lied about it. In the hospital I shouted for her to leave it alone and she turned to the wall and told me to go.

Korczak took my arm and almost tipped us over. 'I just sat there and stared at the faces of the dead children,' he said. 'What was I doing there? What was I looking for?'

A yellow police column jogged by. He looked bothered by his question, so I told him I didn't know.

'What a strange and unsavoury person I was. And am,' he said. He said he wished he'd brought a cigarette. He said he wished he'd eaten his breakfast.

'I'm not sure I know what to do with good times,' he said. 'My mother told me her father was so comfortable with being downtrodden that even when he drew the lucky number in a lottery he kept the news to himself for a week.'

We stepped over a desk blocking the pavement, its drawers open and inkwell broken. He wondered if it was worth sending some boys back to retrieve it. Then he said to remind him that he still needed to talk with

Kramsztyk about the poor quality of his coal. For the rest of the walk back he rolled his head from side to side as if his neck were giving him pain.

★ ★ ★

Auditions for the play were held on the third floor after it had been prepared. Giena was cast as Sudah the flower girl, she told me that night, and I told her that she was already in costume. Jerzyk though he still had his fever was cast as the fakir and had already started working on his magic tricks. They were casting the main role last, Korczak said, and he wanted me to try out for it. I asked what it was and he wondered if I'd read the play and I said no. He said the lead was a boy who was dying and inspired everyone.

'He's the hero?' I said. We were all stripping beds.

'In a way,' he said. 'I think you'd be very good at it.'

'Him?' Madame Stefa asked.

Him, Korczak told her. I said no but was surprised by how happy it made me to have been asked. The next day Korczak announced the star would be a boy named Abrasha, who played the violin.

I was emptying the dustbins with Zygmuś

and another boy and saw Boris coming down the street with a tall woman in a straw hat. It didn't look like he'd seen me and when I got back inside I pushed past the long line of kids waiting for the bathroom and went up to the third floor and climbed inside a painted piece of scenery that said *Lord Mayor's House*. I waited and then heard footsteps and someone came in and shut the door. I could see out the crack beside me.

The woman in the straw hat and Korczak had come in but I didn't see Boris. They searched each other's faces and said it was good to meet again. He told her about the play and she told him how she'd got into the ghetto. She said she'd brought honey cakes and vitamin B for the children and he thanked her.

They were quiet. He asked why she had come and she told him she'd come to get him out of there and he said he thought it was something like that. He asked how she imagined she would do that and she said she belonged to the Żegota movement, which distributed newspapers calling on Poles to help Jews, and they ferried people in and out all the time. He asked if he would be going alone. She said that maybe as many as three or four others could go with him. Then she was quiet again.

I could hear the kids downstairs. Someone tried the door and found it locked and went back down.

'I ask you to accept my help,' the woman said.

'Those of us who were here, if we ever met up after this,' he finally told her. 'How could we look each other in the eye without asking, 'How is it that *you* happened to survive?''

The woman studied her hands. 'Why shouldn't some, if even only a few, be saved?' she asked.

Someone dropped dishes downstairs and kids applauded.

What about the rest, he asked. Could she imagine the ones left behind? ''Pan Doctor is gone. Wait here in the dark,'' he said.

I couldn't tell if the woman was weeping. 'We put out a newspaper,' she said. 'You produce plays. What good does either do? Maybe we should be learning how to handle a rifle instead.'

Korczak laughed. 'I'd love to join the underground but what weapons do they have?' he said. 'One group has a revolver. They showed me.'

'You can come out now,' he called after they sat there a while longer, and I stood up and walked around the scenery. The woman didn't seem surprised to see me. 'You can

216

help me show Maria out,' he said. 'She's one of my most successful graduates.'

'The boy with her is the one I was talking about,' I told him. But he didn't answer and we followed him down the stairs. When I hung back he told me to come on and in the front hall he kissed the woman on both cheeks and then she kissed him on the mouth. Boris stood beside the door and watched them and then looked at me as though he'd never seen me before.

'Please think about what we discussed,' the woman told Korczak.

'I wish I could *stop* thinking about it,' he told her. 'Please thank your friends on the children's behalf.'

'Have you fallen asleep?' he said to me after they'd closed the door behind them. 'Are you just going to stand there and squint?'

In the kitchen he was stopped by a little girl. 'You're the tenth person to ask me about the honey cakes,' he told her. 'Do you think there are no problems to solve other than the honey cakes?' She went to Madame Stefa, who gave her a hug. 'Do I need to have eyes in the back of my head to keep everyone working?' he called to the group.

★ ★ ★

He read his letters aloud to himself in the early morning when he thought everyone else was asleep, so that night I stopped on the stairs and watched from the darkness. I had spent the day mystified by why Boris had acted the way he had.

Korczak held his letter up to the light and read: 'To the Editor of the *Jewish Gazette*: Dear Mr Editor! Thank you for your favorable evaluation of the Orphanage's activity. But: 'Love Plato, yet love more the truth.' The Orphanage was not, is not, and will never be Korczak's Orphanage. The man is too small, too weak, too poor, and too dimwitted to gather, feed, warm, protect, and initiate into life almost two hundred children. This great task — this Herculean task — '

He stopped and cleared his throat and laid the paper down and made some marks on it. ' — has been accomplished through the collective efforts of hundreds of people of goodwill and enlightened minds and insight. As well as by the children themselves.'

He stopped again, still looking at the paper. 'Not having any confidence, we are disinclined to promise. Nevertheless, we are assured that an hour of a thinker and a poet's beautiful fairy tale will provide an experience of the highest order in the scale of feelings. Therefore, we all together invite you — ' he said. 'We take this occasion to invite you . . . '

He stood and turned from his writing, then sat down on his bed.

Three weeks of rehearsals were scheduled on the posting board and the performance date was listed as Saturday, July 18. Those who weren't involved were invited to contribute their opinions when not occupied with chores. The night before everyone got food poisoning and those staff members not throwing up or huddled over chamber pots moved through the darkness with jugs of limewater and morphine for the worst off. Mietek had a nightmare about his mother that was so terrible he shrieked and screamed he was burning up and dying of thirst until Korczak shouted into his face that he would throw him down the stairs and out into the street if he didn't quieten down.

'That seemed to have worked,' Madame Stefa told him later, while they were soaking up the sick with rags.

'Our director shouts and therefore is in command,' he told her.

'He was upsetting everyone,' she said.

'I'm the son of a madman,' he said. 'To this day the thought is a torment to me.'

The next morning the main hall looked like a battlefield, but by five that evening the performers had pulled themselves together and got into costume.

The audience filled the room and even with the windows open it was so hot that everyone fanned themselves with programs. It smelled of the night before.

Korczak welcomed the guests and told them that an author from India would speak through the mouths of Jewish children in a Polish ghetto. The lights went out and whispers and sounds came from behind the curtain and the kids in the front rows pushed and shoved. The play once it started seemed made for the smaller ones. Abrasha played a sick boy not allowed to leave his room. In the lights his one big eyebrow made him look angry. He had conversations with his doctor and his mother and his stepfather and a watchman on the street and with the mayor and with a fakir and with a flower girl. Then somebody named the Royal Physician came dressed all in white and Abrasha told everyone that he no longer felt any pain and when the boy playing his stepfather asked why they were putting out the lights in his room and opening the curtains and how the starlight would help, Giena stepped forward as the flower girl and held out her hands and said, 'Be quiet, unbeliever.' And it was as if the entire audience had decided to listen. The kid next to me who'd begun to scratch himself stopped.

The physician said Abrasha was asleep and Gieńa asked when he would awake and the physician said as soon as the king came to call him from this world. And she asked if he would whisper a word from her into Abrasha's ear and when he asked her what he should say, she said, before all the lights went out, to tell him she had not forgotten him.

Everyone said they were very moved by the play. An old woman in a Chinaman's hat told Korczak that he was a genius and could work miracles in a rat hole. He told her that must have been why the others had all been given the palaces.

★ ★ ★

Four days later there was noise on the street early in the morning and in the kitchen Madame Stefa congratulated Korczak on his birthday and handed him a cup of something she'd cooked, and then gave a cry when through the window she saw the lines of blue police and Lithuanians and Ukrainians in black with brown leather collars. Boris had taught me the uniforms. A boy who carried messages from the hospital came in gasping and panting. He said the children there were being evacuated to the Umschlagplatz and apparently getting dumped next to the tracks in their hospital gowns. Korczak got some money from a hiding place behind the stove and ran out the door while the boy was still talking.

I ran after him. Where would I go if he disappeared? I collided with a group running by and a man with a valise knocked me down. Everyone was running out of the courtyard of the building next door and those in the back were being whipped and trying to push forward. We were carried down the street like a river and collected in a blockade. I couldn't see if Korczak was with us. We were pulled into lines of four and shoved onto our haunches in the street. One of the Lithuanians demonstrated and clubbed anybody who didn't obey on the head. We crouched there while more and more people joined us, everyone wailing and calling to friends and relatives in the crowd. They were shouting, 'Where are my children? Tell them I'm leaving.' Or that they had a sewing machine or worked at Többens's. The yellow police took the sides of the column and the Lithuanians the back and they stood everyone up and got us moving again.

I worked over to the closest yellow

policeman and everyone was shouting at him at once, giving him their names, asking if there was anything he could do, asking him to tell their wives or sons or husbands where they were. He shouted for them all to shut up and when I got close enough to ask if he knew Lejkin he hit me in the face with his stick.

A little girl helped me up and was crying that they had to send her home so she could take care of her younger sister. I asked why she was telling me and a woman took her hand and pulled her away. People were fished from the mob or jumped into doorways or dropped down cellar stairs when the policemen were distracted or willing to look the other way.

A blue policeman dragged a girl into the crowd from an apartment we passed and I stepped through the door before he slammed it shut. The girl called, 'Mr Policeman!' and then disappeared. The inner entry doors were locked but I held the outer ones together with my arm through the handles. I held them tight until everything had passed by and the street got quiet.

I cracked the door open and saw a shoe on its side in the street. My cheek was numb. My arm holding the door was shaking. I heard banging metal and opened the door wider.

A German down the street was hammering the bolt of his rifle with the butt of his bayonet. I could see spectacles on the cobblestones near him. Nearer to me a girl lay on her back.

I shut the door but could still hear her cries. The building around me was silent. When I finally looked out the doors again she was dead and the street was empty except for her and her spectacles. Even the shoe was gone. The sun hurt my eyes.

The next street over I could follow the trail of suitcases and scattered hats. Window shutters swung squeaking. One banged against a wall. Feathers still floated around from torn-up bedding.

I started back to the orphanage and two looters passed carrying a clothes wringer. On Twarda a German was poking a pile of clothes with a long stick and I hid and waited for him to leave. On Sienna the Ukrainians sat with their backs to the ghetto wall, tired and drinking with their shirts open. I got into the orphanage through the courtyard.

The kids were all in the middle of the upstairs room with the blackout paper still up on the windows. Everyone was together on the floor. Madame Stefa hugged me but Korczak stayed with his arms around Mietek and another little girl who was asleep.

Madame Stefa told me to clean my face.

Some kids were whispering but most were listening. There was shouting and whistles and boots running by outside. Every so often someone got up to use the chamber pot.

We stayed like for that a day and a night. There was no dinner. No one lit any lamps. Once it got late Korczak stood up and weaved through the tangle of sleepers and lifted a corner of the blackout paper on one of the windows. He stood over Madame Stefa, who was asleep with her head back and mouth open, and raised a finger to his lips when he saw me looking. We watched each other until the sun came up and it was like the city outside was gone except for the occasional shot or voice calling in the darkness.

★ ★ ★

After that Korczak went out every day and never let anyone else go with him. When he returned he told whoever wanted to listen what was happening as far as he could tell. The smallest kids held the hands of older ones, proud to have been included.

He said members of the Jewish Council had been arrested and their families held hostage. He said a proclamation had appeared announcing that all of the Jews would be resettled outside of Warsaw and only a few workers were to remain exempt and also that those who reported voluntarily would receive three kilos of bread and one of jam. He told Madame Stefa that only the Germans would have chosen to begin this on Tisha B'Av and when a kid asked why, he explained that Tisha B'Av was a fast day commemorating Nebuchadnezzar the king of Babylon's destruction of the First Temple and the Roman emperor Titus's destruction of the Second. He said they were going street by street and doors that were locked or bolted were broken down and the streets emptied one day were being revisited on the next to catch those hiding in places already searched.

He told of how he'd saved an old student by pulling her from a Jewish policeman and shouting that he'd saved the policeman's daughter that afternoon and so the policeman had let them go, but that he *hadn't* saved the policeman's daughter, not that the man could have ever known for sure.

He said he'd been thrown onto one of the roundup wagons and then a street later had been recognized by another yellow policeman who'd helped him down and warned him not to play the hero or it would get everyone killed. If they had to give up an arm or a leg to save the body, so be it. And if the Jews helped out, wouldn't that mean fewer casualties and less brutality?

Was this how they were all supposed to ride off into the unknown, Madame Stefa asked, with no fresh clothes, no bundles, not even a piece of bread?

So many kids were crying that Korczak said the policeman had assured him that the orphanage was so famous that the Germans would never touch it. Everyone else was running about frantically trying to get work papers, and men who'd been captains of industry were now overjoyed to sweep a factory yard and everybody said the brush-makers' workshops were the best, because they were controlled by the army, or that Többens's workshop on Prosta Street was, because he was Göring's brother-in-law, so everyone wanted the green pass from Többens. But no one knew what worked and what didn't, and what seemed secure one day was a soap bubble the next. He said that while he'd been trapped on the wagon a German had told a woman whose papers featured all the proper seals and signatures that she was an imbecile and the best document that *she* could hope to find was a cellar.

At night we stayed quiet and listened for the patrols. We could hear muffled sounds of people coming out of their hiding places for water and food. When someone cried or called out down below the windows we weren't allowed to look.

Almost no one was sleeping. Korczak and Madame Stefa talked on the third floor when it was very late. Sometimes I listened from the stairs and sometimes I didn't. Their voices were so low I couldn't hear everything. He told her the shooting on Ogrodowa Street had gone on all day to accommodate those who hadn't been at home earlier. She asked how he knew that and he asked how anyone knew anything. He said if people had survived they'd probably been hiding whenever something happened.

He said children had walked to the Umschlagplatz in order to travel with their families. The lucky ones left behind were stealing from empty homes since it couldn't be stealing if there were no longer any owners. He said that the Ukrainians at the end of the day reminded him of farmers at the end of a harvest.

★ ★ ★

The next day he came back so upset he wouldn't let anyone see him until Madame Stefa talked to him alone. Outside we heard the horns of police vans and whistles and the sound of people running.

He told her he'd gone all the way to the Umschlagplatz to find Esterka and got past the Ukrainians and Germans and Jewish police and found her and had tried to bring her to the hospital. At the gate he asked a blue policeman if he could help his assistant who was vital to his orphanage and the Pole said he knew very well that he couldn't and while another Pole and a Jewish policeman dragged Esterka away Korczak stood there and let it happen and thanked the Pole for his kind words. This was what it had come to, Korczak said: he'd now been trained to be thankful for even that.

Kids tried to get by me on the stairs and asked what Korczak and Madame Stefa were talking about up there but I said I didn't know. I couldn't hear what else they said. Finally I heard him tell her they had responsibilities downstairs and to remember that if Miss Esterka didn't return she'd assist others in the meantime, just as she had made herself so useful here.

★ ★ ★

The next morning a runner from the Judenrat told him about Czerniaków's suicide. His secretary had found him dead in his office chair. Czerniaków had written notes to his wife and to the Judenrat. The runner showed the Judenrat note to Korczak, who read it and refolded it and handed it back, and the runner left.

When Madame Stefa heard they stood facing each other, their foreheads touching.

The rest of the morning other staff members gave what orders needed to be given. Korczak and Madame Stefa sat at the kitchen table over a single cold glass of tea. 'The easy way out,' she finally said.

'He gave up a visa to Palestine to serve his community,' he answered.

Neither of them left the kitchen when Zygmuś told me there were two boys outside who wanted to see me and when I opened the front door a crack Boris pulled me out and another boy shut the door behind me. I was so scared I couldn't hear what Boris was saying at first and finally the other boy slapped me and got my attention. He asked if I knew the interior of the Żelazna Street house, the one the Germans had set up, and asked me to describe its rooms and then seemed satisfied when I did. He asked how often I went there and at what times of day and whether the Germans guarded the doors. He said they needed me to let them know from the inside when it was a good time to pay a visit and I asked who they were and he said his group and when I asked who was in his group he told me it was none of my fucking business.

Boris still had me by the shirtfront and I said why should I do anything for them and Boris said because if I didn't he would kill me and I said then he should just go ahead and kill me. They stared at me for a while until the other boy asked what I wanted and I had to think. Then I told him I wanted Korczak saved. And Madame Stefa too, if that's what Korczak wanted. Boris snorted. The other boy thought about it and then said yes, he could arrange for this if I gave him what he wanted and that I'd be hearing from him soon. Then they left.

That night Gieńa's older brother Samuel visited before curfew and she threw herself on him and the kids gathered around and stared. Madame Stefa and Korczak watched with their arms folded. Gieńa's brother told her he had to talk to Korczak and Madame Stefa and she waited with her friends in the main room while he sat with them in the kitchen. The glass was still where they'd left it, though someone had drunk the tea. I sat in the hall by the doorway.

The brother told them he'd heard the orphanage wouldn't be touched but that he couldn't be sure and had promised his mother to watch over his sister and that lately his nightmares had convinced him they should be together, given what was happening. But he hardly knew the couple he lived with and worried that his sister would be terrified to be alone all day while he worked.

He waited but Korczak was silent. Madame Stefa finally said they too believed the orphanage would be safe and that taking children away wasn't good for the group's morale, though this was his decision.

So he talked with his sister and she couldn't decide but eventually left with him the next morning. But the morning after that he brought her back, because of what she'd heard when she'd been locked alone in his room. He brought her back in time for breakfast and sat her at her place. He wiped his eyes and promised he would visit when he could, and she told him he'd been very helpful and should take care of himself. Then she picked up her spoon and turned away. After he left Madame Stefa asked why Korczak was waiting tables and he told her he liked to keep occupied and by picking up soup bowls and spoons and plates he could see who was sitting next to whom. And who was most alone.

★   ★   ★

That night after even Korczak had fallen asleep there was a low rapping at the back door and when I took the lamp over to it and threw the bolt open Boris shoved me back and he and the other boy stepped in and shut the door behind them.

'How can we help you gentlemen?' Korczak said. He was in his nightshirt and without his glasses.

'Come into the kitchen,' the other boy said, and took the lamp from me and led us there.

They sat at the table and we stood in front of them. 'Hello again,' I said to Boris.

'Hello,' Boris said.

'Yes, it's nice to be back,' the other boy said. Then he told Korczak that representatives of the youth movements had met and established the Jewish Fighting Organization and had decided their first task was to inform everyone that the deportations were to a camp at Treblinka where everyone was to be gassed. They were already distributing flyers but the flyers were being destroyed by the Judenrat, who viewed them as a German provocation intended as a pretext to shoot everyone.

'If everyone's being gassed then how has this information reached you?' Korczak asked.

One or two who'd escaped from the trains came back to the ghetto every week, the boy told him.

'And these people are reliable?' Korczak asked. 'How did they achieve this feat?' I asked if he wanted me to fetch his glasses and he said no.

'In my case I managed to tear the barbed wire from the window and wriggle through,' the boy said. When he saw Korczak's face he added, 'I'm not Hercules. Others ahead of me worked at it and ran out of time.'

They stared at each other. I thought: that's what I would do. I'd climb over heads if I had to.

'Others kicked out floorboards or sideboards,' the boy said.

'While the train was still moving?' I asked, but the boy gave me such a look that I shut up.

'Are there no guards on the trains?' Korczak asked.

'There are guards,' the boy said. 'Some who get away are shot and some aren't.'

Korczak seemed unsurprised by any of this. 'And you're a member of this fighting organization?' he asked.

The boy said they'd come for two reasons and the first was to help Korczak escape.

The Polish underground was always offering to help him escape, Korczak told him, but he always said no unless they could take everyone.

'They want you because you're the only one they consider a Pole,' the boy said. 'But we want to get you out not just because you're the famous Dr Korczak. We want you to help spread the word about what's going on.'

'Why would anyone listen to me?' Korczak said.

The boy didn't answer. 'Tell him,' he said to me.

'Tell me what?' Korczak said. And all three of them looked at me.

'They're also here because they want my help,' I told him. 'I said if they wanted me to help them they had to do this for me.'

'Do what for you?' Korczak asked. His expression was so surprised and disappointed that I had to look away.

'Get you out,' Boris said. He said the Germans were directing their resettlement from an office on Żelazna. He said Lejkin was the Jew in charge and that I had worked as an informer for him and the Gestapo, which meant I could get inside. And since I could get inside, then I could help them attack it when the time came.

'You want him to help you attack their office?' Korczak asked.

'His price was getting you out,' the other boy said.

'When was all this arranged?' Korczak asked me.

'They came to the home yesterday,' I told him. 'I talked with them on the front step.'

'When did you imagine you would do this?' he asked me, in the voice he used when he talked to the Germans.

'He'll have to come now,' Boris said.

'I'm not doing anything until he's out of the ghetto,' I told them.

'Do you have guns? Do you have bombs?' Korczak asked.

'We're getting guns. We're getting bombs,' Boris said.

'From where?' Korczak asked.

Boris finally told him that his plan was for me to bring him to the wall at the end of Prózna Street at four the following night and there would be a ladder and someone waiting on the other side to take him out of the city.

Korczak walked to the sink and stood with his back to us. 'I'm waiting to speak until I'm not so angry,' he said.

The other boy moved the tea glass from spot to spot on the table like a chess piece. When I looked at Boris he only shrugged.

Korczak turned around. 'And all the children in this orphanage?' he said to me. 'I'm going to leave them now, when they have so little time left?'

I put my hands on my face. 'I just wanted to save you,' I said.

The other boy said, 'Boris chose the spot along the wall from your smuggling days. He picked a good one.'

'When they argue with one another the children have a saying,' Korczak finally told us. 'They say, 'I'll give you away in a bag.''

'Tell them the truth,' the boy said. 'Tell them we can't save them.'

'Tell them they're all just on their own?' Korczak asked, and his anger surprised even them.

'They *are* all on their own,' the boy said.

'They're *not* all on their own,' Korczak said. None of us could look at anyone else.

'So you won't go?' the boy finally said to Korczak. 'And you won't help us if he doesn't go?' he said to me.

My hands were still on my face, Madame Stefa was now standing in the doorway.

'Maybe he'll change his mind,' I said.

'But you have to come now,' Boris said.

'And just leave him? And everyone else?' I asked.

'Aron's not a violent boy,' Madame Stefa said. She cleared her throat and said it again.

'Sh'maya? Don't tell me about Sh'maya,' Boris said. 'Because of him my two best friends are dead. Sh'maya doesn't care about anyone but himself. Do you, Sh'maya?'

The other boy got up from the table and looked sad when he put the glass in the sink. 'So you're going to do as you're told,' he said to Korczak. 'And make everything simpler for the Germans.'

'Gentlemen, it's been a long day,' Korczak told them. Madame Stefa stepped over and put an arm on his shoulder.

'And now he's crying,' Boris said to the boy about me, as though he'd predicted it. I put my fists atop my head as if that would help.

The Jews could fight better than anyone knew, the boy said. He said there was an anti-aircraft post near Mława during the first days of the war when everyone else had run away during an air raid and the Jews had shot down seventeen planes. 'Seventeen planes!' he said.

'You won't go?' I asked Korczak. He looked away.

'Make yourself useful,' Boris finally said to me.

'Make up for what you've done,' the other boy said.

'I've never been useful,' I told them. 'And I can't make up for what I've done.'

They both stared at me. 'I never thought he'd help,' Boris said, pointing at Korczak. 'But I thought you might.'

The other boy looked at me with hatred. 'We have no chance without someone on the inside,' he said to Korczak. 'Tell him that.'

'It's his decision,' Korczak said.

Lice and bedbugs swarmed around on my head and chest. I raked my hands over them. 'Can I take a day to think about it?' I asked.

'You don't have a day,' the boy said.

'Then no,' I told him.

★   ★   ★

Korczak went up to his room after they left and Madame Stefa followed him. I sat below in the dark with the sleeping kids until I couldn't stand it anymore and climbed the stairs.

They were sitting together. He had pulled the blackout paper down from one of the windows and the sheets on all the beds gave off a pale light. The paper was still in his hand and when he crumpled it only a few of the sicker kids stirred.

'What a marvellous big moon over this camp of helpless pilgrims,' he said to himself. It was as sad as I'd ever seen him.

'I'm sorry,' I said from across the room.

He nodded. 'Do you even understand why I'm so angry?' he said.

'I just wanted you to be safe,' I said. But he didn't seem to have heard.

'Can I get you anything?' Madame Stefa asked him after a minute.

He shook his head. 'Sit with us,' he said without looking at me, and patted the sheet.

I went past the other beds and sat at the foot of his next to Madame Stefa and after he laid down we did too, though our feet were still on the floor. We listened to his breathing.

'Did you know I met Madame Stefa on a trip to Switzerland when I was still a student?' he asked. I shook my head but he couldn't see. She made an amused sound.

'I told her on our first meeting during a long exchange on a park bench that I was the son of a mental patient but was going to become the Karl Marx of children,' he said.

'Thank you,' I told him, 'for calling me over.'

'She was very self-assured,' he said.

'I'm still self-assured,' she told him.

'She was eating an unripe pear,' he said, and she stretched an arm in his direction. I felt his knee under the sheet.

'Always at the back of your mind is the question of what you'll do when they finally do come,' he said after we'd been lying there for a few minutes. He touched his glass and his cigarettes and then fell asleep.

★　★　★

When he woke up I did too and he propped himself up on his elbows. It was early. Gieńa was in her nightshirt under the window. 'Good morning,' he said to her.

'Good morning,' she said back.

'Smile,' he told her, and she did. He said that today he thought he'd like a breakfast of sausage, ham, and buns. Madame Stefa got to her feet and walked to the staircase and shouted 'Boys! Breakfast! Get up!' and down below we could hear beds moved and the wooden tables pushed together and the pot being filled in the kitchen. Then there were two whistle blasts and men at the front and back doors shouted, 'All Jews out! All Jews out!'

Gieńa put a hand to her mouth. Madame Stefa ran downstairs. Korczak struggled into his clothes and I followed him down once he'd stuffed his feet into his shoes.

Madame Stefa was in the main room trying

241

to keep the kids calm. She shook some who were making too much noise. The Germans and Ukrainians were still shouting. Korczak looked out the kitchen window and saw something that made him pull me out the back door into the courtyard with him.

It was filled with men standing around: five or six SS, a line of Ukrainians, and two more of yellow police. The SS and Ukrainians were wearing long overcoats in the heat and sweating and yelling for water, Lejkin was bent over with his hands on his hips in front of his police. Korczak asked him what was happening and Lejkin told him to get everyone together. Korczak asked again and Lejkin repeated himself.

When Korczak told him he needed time to allow the children to pack up, Lejkin said that he had twenty minutes.

'Explain to him,' Korczak said to me. 'Tell him that I need more time.'

'He needs more time,' I said to Lejkin.

Lejkin looked at me. 'Ten minutes,' he said.

Korczak pushed back inside and clapped his hands for everyone's attention. Madame Stefa and the other staff members worked on getting those who were most upset to listen to him. He asked two boys to close the doors and when some Ukrainians tried to stop them he shouted, 'We still have five minutes,' so they allowed it.

Once the doors were shut the kids pushed forward as if whoever was closest to him would be the safest. I pushed forward myself. I was so panicked I was just calling, 'Pan Doctor! Pan Doctor!' Mietek held my shirt tail to keep his position. His head was so full of lice it was like he had gray hair.

Korczak said it had been claimed this home was so filled with the well-behaved that at times you wouldn't know there was a child in the house. He said his mother had told him he had no ambition because it always had been the same to him whether he played with his own kind or the caretaker's children and that there was no one with whom he would rather undertake what we were all about to do. He said where we were going there'd be no card-playing, no sunbathing, and no rest. When some of the kids made noises he said he was telling us this because he'd spent his entire life demanding respect for the child and it was time to practice what he preached. More kids made noise and he quieted them with a hand gesture. He said not to forget that Moses himself had been a child under a death sentence. He told everyone of a time he'd convinced Jerzyk not to cover some ants with dirt. And who knows, he said: maybe even now those ants were back at their home, telling the story of how they survived.

He told us to arrange ourselves in lines of four and the staff members helped. It took all of the time we had left. The doors burst open before we were finished and the shouting started again.

Korczak waited for it to stop and then said he was already so proud of us that his heart was bursting. And who was to say that if anyone had a chance of surviving it couldn't be us? And he said he'd use his old magic, we would see, to wheedle bread and potatoes and medicine for everyone. And that he'd be with us for whatever lay ahead.

Madame Stefa was holding one of the sicker five-year-olds, and handed another to Korczak. He hefted her in front of everyone and said Romcia would be our standard-bearer. Along with Jerzyk who had spared the ants. He asked one of the staff to hand Jerzyk the bright-green flag with the Jewish star and two older kids helped him with the harness.

Mietek was still in his rotten boots with his dead brother's prayer book. Abrasha with his eyebrow had his violin in its case. Zygmuś was bare-handed. Other kids held toys or cups. Most had put their caps on.

At the front door an SS man held a clipboard and took a roll call that took several minutes. The kids packed in tighter on

Korczak. The SS man called out the door when he was finished that a hundred and ninety-two children and ten adults were accounted for. Korczak told the staff to spread themselves out and take every fifth row of four but Dora and Balbina had trouble finding their spots. Dora said that all her life she'd had to be first and just this once wanted to take her place farther back. Balbina said she'd never seen anything like it in her entire life and this was the first time she'd ever gone on a trip without knowing where she was going. They were still arguing when he led us out into the sunlight.

It was hot. The pavements were so full that we had to walk in the street. Madame Stefa asked why this was and Korczak told her everyone was now required to stand in front of their homes when such operations were taking place.

It was a gigantic procession, a rag parade, everyone staggering and squinting in the daylight, most carrying spoons and bowls. Some of the kids were cheered just to be walking all together.

The sky was hazy. We were the only ones making noise, with our feet. Everyone watching was quiet. We went up Sosnowa, Śliska, and Komitetowa. After a few streets people called, 'Stay well!' or said goodbye to particular kids by name.

All the shoes on the cobblestones made a clopping sound. There was a lot of dust. When we turned up Twarda the sun was in our eyes. Dora started singing 'Though the Storm Howls Around Us' and held up her hand to block the sun while she sang. She didn't have a very strong voice.

She went on alone for half a block before Madame Stefa and Balbina and the rest of the staff and finally Korczak and the kids joined in. I started singing my younger brother's name.

'Those aren't the words,' Zygmuś told me.

'What do you care,' I said. One of the Germans escorting the procession pretended to sing along.

The song stopped at Grzybowska Square when we saw all the others. We took a rest while the Germans tried to organize everyone. Korczak put Romcia down. People in the square looked as shocked to see him as he was to see them. We stood with a big group of older girls from the School of Nursing who were all dressed in their uniforms, Korczak told the woman leading them that he'd managed to secure a special wagon for his children.

When they got us moving again at the intersection it was like two floods merging. As the crowd got bigger people had to work harder to stay in their groups. We took over the pavements and the Jews looking on had to retreat into doorways or courtyards or else get carried along. Almost everyone was carrying sacks and suitcases or dragging bundles, knocking into the kids and mixing into our lines. Zygmuś got pushed down a side street covered with abandoned bags and luggage and had to fight his way back into the procession. People shouted they'd forgotten their ration cards and had to go back or asked if there'd be water up ahead and if the yellow police had gone deaf.

At Krochmalna an SS man with a cap shaped like a horse's saddle watched us go by, Gieńa took my hand and told me she'd hidden some bread in her bag.

At Chłodna Street there was another slowdown because kids fell going up the steps. The boards on the top of the bridge bent and creaked under everyone's weight. Somewhere outside the wall an Aryan tram clanged its bell. I could see our gang's old gate. Jerzyk waved his flag when he got to the top of the bridge. He spat down at the street below.

We kept walking. We'd been walking since seven. We were all walking and swaying, walking and swaying, walking and swaying.

The sun was now straight overhead. My ears were ringing. Kids stumbled and fell into one another. How were they doing this with no food or water? I felt like I was flooding with something inside.

We stopped twice on Zamenhofa. Every so often someone called Korczak's name in surprise. The twine on my shoes came undone and I stepped out of them. Some kids had to be pulled off the pavement when we started moving again. They cried they were thirsty or wanted to rest or needed to go to the bathroom. Korczak was still in the front and still carrying someone. We passed my old apartment and I saw my house. I saw my window. Boris stood with his arms folded at the front door, next to his mother.

The gate where the ghetto ended opened well before we got there. Germans and Ukrainians stood in lines on either side of it with clubs and guns and dogs.

Everyone was shoved through and funnelled across tram tracks that opened onto a dirt field by a railway siding. Barbed wire wrapped around a cement post tore my sleeve. Jews already there were weeping and sitting and standing in the hot sun. Clothes and soup spoons and toys and sick were spilled around us. People shouted and hugged when they found someone. Some sat in circles facing one another and others wandered around spattered with blood.

Korczak led us to the far end and sat the smallest kids against the wall for shade. He got some men to move to make room.

He sat with the boys and Madame Stefa with the girls. One of the boys asked what would happen next and I heard him say, 'Now we're going on a trip to the forest.' A yellow policeman took the flag from Jerzyk and tossed it over the wall. Ukrainians came by saying that whoever had good boots should give them up since they'd be taken later anyway.

Mietek was still holding my shirt tail, The German Witossek stood over us and reintroduced himself to Korczak. His uniform was soaked with sweat even through the empty sleeve that was pinned up and he said that wool was unsuitable for this kind of heat. He took off his cap and wiped his forehead with his sleeve and Korczak turned his attention to the children.

Witossek apologized for the necessity of what had to happen and said he hoped Korczak understood the necessity was one thing and the people who had to carry it out were another. He said he wanted the good doctor to know that what was going to happen was going to happen and that how everyone chose to face it would be the point.

'I agree with you,' Korczak said.

I heard someone singing a song about the king of Siberia. 'Pisher!' I shouted. 'Pisher!' I stood up and looked around.

The Ukrainians and the yellow police began loading those closest onto the train cars. People were screaming as they were pulled to their feet. Germans lounged against the wall and watched. Some teased the kids nearby. Witossek put his cap back on and walked over to join them.

The Ukrainians and the yellow police kicked and pushed everyone they could into the open doorways. The Ukrainians used their rifle butts as well. Arms and hands stretched out the little window through the barbed wire. When it looked like there was no more room in a car a German walked over with his pistol and fired into the crowd and everyone near who was shot fell backwards and another six or seven people were shoved into the space.

The train was filled and the doors banged shut and the Jews inside screamed until it left. Dust hung in the air from where the ramps had been kicked down.

Korczak put his hands on Abrasha's shoulders and told him something and other boys leaned in to listen. Madame Stefa put her arms around two girls. A Ukrainian bent over Gieńa and fingered her beads as she sat there with her hands in her lap.

The yellow police gathered around a white enamel pail and took turns cooling off with ladles of water, some pouring it over their heads. Lejkin took the ladle and I put Mietek's hand on Zygmuś's shirt tail and worked my way over to him.

'Look who's here,' Lejkin said.

'I know where all the smugglers' holes are,' I told him.

'So do I,' Lejkin said. The headband of his cap was so soaked you couldn't read the lettering. He poured water down his shirt-front.

'I know where all the smugglers are,' I told him.

'So do I,' he said.

'No you don't,' I said.

He looked at me like he'd been swindled before. 'So I get you out of here and you'll deliver those people to me?' he said.

I pointed to Korczak and Madame Stefa and said, 'You get them out of here and I'll deliver those people to you.'

'Ah,' he said. 'Well, a lot of people would like to get him out of here.' He said something to the policeman beside him and we walked over to Korczak.

'Pan Doctor,' he said.

'Mr Lejkin,' Korczak said. He didn't have his glasses and the sun made him squint.

'Another train is on its way,' Lejkin told him.

'Another train is always on its way,' Korczak said. He was shaking.

'This young man seems to think you should be saved,' Lejkin told him.

'I think we all should be saved,' Korczak said.

'It's possible that could be arranged,' Lejkin told him.

Korczak looked up. 'And how would that happen?' he said.

'You'd have to come with me and ask the commanding officer,' Lejkin said.

'And where is he?' Korczak asked.

'Not far,' Lejkin said. 'A ten-minute walk.'

'Will you guarantee they won't be taken away while I'm gone?' Korczak asked.

'You're joking, yes?' Lejkin said. 'You're making a joke?'

'Then no,' Korczak told him.

'You might be able to get *everyone* out,' I said.

'So I should leave them here, all by themselves, in this place?' he asked me.

'I'll watch them. You could hurry,' I said.

'You'll watch them,' he said.

'I'll watch them,' I said.

'And can you imagine what it would be like for *them* if the next train comes back while I'm gone?' he said.

'Please,' I said.

'Please what?' he said.

'*Listen* to me,' I shouted. But the truth was I couldn't imagine anything. I always imagined myself, put upon. I never imagined anything else. And the next train sounded its whistle and ground around the curve into view and there was more screaming and calling out of names until its brakes drowned everyone out.

Korczak turned his attention back to his boys and Madame Stefa stood up and walked over to him. Girls hung on to her skirt. Korczak held out his hand and she squeezed it. Zygmuś and Mietek squatted wet-eyed and miserable. 'I pissed myself,' Zygmuś told me as though that were the worst of all. By the train cars the shouting started up again.

'Everyone up,' Korczak said. 'Rows of four.'

I wailed and shook and jabbered until someone took my hands from my face. It was Korczak. 'Stop,' he said. But I wouldn't.

'I never showed you my Declaration of Children's Rights,' he said. Behind him the kids had collected their things, boys and girls together, and had got into their rows. Zygmuś was pulling at the back of his pants. A yellow policeman beside him started to weep.

'There isn't a bit of me left in sound health,' Korczak said to himself.

He bent farther down until he was close enough for me to smell him. He put his hands behind my head and lowered his forehead to mine. I was blubbering and got his face wet but he only drew closer. ''The child has the right to respect,'' he said. ''The child has the right to develop. The child has the right to be. The child has the right to grieve. The child has the right to learn. And the child has the right to make mistakes.''

Nothing is definitively known about the last hours of Janusz Korczak and his staff members and his children, and for some time after the war it was said that he and Stefa and some of the orphans had been saved and that they had been seen in villages throughout Poland. Accounts vary, but most likely they were deported to Treblinka on the afternoon of August 5, 1942. Dr Imfried Eberl, the commander of the camp, reported to his superiors that at the time Treblinka was in such a state of overtaxed chaos that mountains of corpses confronted the new arrivals, and therefore maintaining any kind of deception on the way to the gas chambers was nearly impossible.

Acknowledgments

My main object here, to quote Marguerite Yourcenar in her Bibliographical Note to her *Memoirs of Hadrian*, has been 'to approach inner reality, if possible, through careful examination of what the documents themselves afford,' and so this novel could not have existed, or would have existed in a much diminished form, without critically important contributions from the following sources: Janusz Korczak's *Ghetto Diary; The Selected Works of Janusz Korczak*, Martin Wolins, ed.; Aaron Zeitlin's prose poem 'The Last Walk of Janusz Korczak'; Emmanuel Ringelblum's *Notes from the Warsaw Ghetto*, Jacob Sloan, ed.; Barbara Engelking and Jacek Leociak's *The Warsaw Ghetto: A Guide to the Perished City*; Marta Markowska's *The Ringelblum Archive: Annihilation — Day by Day*; Bogdan Wojdowski's *Bread for the Departed*; and Dawid Rubinowicz's *The Diary of Dawid Rubinowicz*.

I'm also hugely indebted to *To Live with Honor and Die with Honor: Selected Documents from the Warsaw Ghetto Underground Archives O.S. (Oneg Shabbath)*,

Joseph Kermish, ed.; *The Warsaw Ghetto Oyneg-Ringelblum Archive Catalog and Guide*, Robert Moses Shapiro and Tadeusz Epsztein, eds; *The Diary of Dawid Sierakowiak*, Alan Adelson, ed.; *The Yad Vashem Encyclopedia of the Ghettos During the Holocaust*, Guy Miron and Shlomit Shulhani, eds; *Words to Outlive Us: Eyewitness Accounts from the Warsaw Ghetto*, Michal Grynberg, ed.; *Awakening Lives: Autobiographies of Jewish Youth in Poland Before the Holocaust*, Jeffrey Shandler, ed.; *From a Ruined Garden: The Memorial Books of Polish Jewry*, Jack Kugelmass and Jonathan Boyarin, eds; *The Last Eyewitness: Children of the Holocaust Speak, Volume 1*, Wiktoria Śliwowska, ed., *Volume 2*, Jakub Gutenbaum and Agnieszka Latała, eds; *Hunger Disease: Studies by the Jewish Physicians in the Warsaw Ghetto*, Myron Winick, MD, ed.; *The Diary of Samuel Golfard and the Holocaust in Galicia*, Wendy Lower, ed.; *The Warsaw Diary of Adam Czerniakow*, Raul Hilberg, Stanislaw Staroń, and Josef Kermisz, Eds; and Betty Jean Lifton's *The King of Children*.

I also found crucially useful Agnieszka Witkowska-Krych's article 'The Last Journey of the Residents and Staff of the Warsaw Orphanage'; Lucjan Dobroszycki's *The*

Chronicle of the Łódz Ghetto, 1941–1944; Leni Yahil's *The Holocaust: The Fate of European Jewry 1932–1945*; Kurt Grübler's *Journey Through the Night: Jakob Littner's Holocaust Memoir*; Adina Blady Szwajger's *I Remember Nothing More: The Warsaw Children's Hospital and the Jewish Resistance*; Abraham Lewin's *A Cup of Tears: A Diary of the Warsaw Ghetto*, Antony Polonsky, ed.; Raul Hilberg's *The Destruction of the European Jews*; Günther Schwarberg's *In the Ghetto of Warsaw: Heinrich Jöst's Photographs*; Hanna Krall's *Shielding the Flame: An Intimate Conversation with Dr Marek Edelman, the Last Surviving Leader of the Warsaw Ghetto Uprising*; Naomi Samson's *Hide: A Child's View of the Holocaust*; Willy Georg's *In the Warsaw Ghetto: Summer 1941*; Jürgen Stroop's *The Stroop Report*; Larry Stillman and Morris Goldner's *A Match Made in Hell: The Jewish Boy and the Polish Outlaw Who Defied the Nazis*; Manny Drukier's *Carved in Stone: Holocaust Years — A Boy's Tale*; Bernard Gotfryd's *Anton the Dove Fancier and Other Tales of the Holocaust*; Lizzie Collingham's *The Taste of War: World War Hand the Battle for Food*; Joseph Ziemian's *The Cigarette Sellers of Three Crosses Square*; George

Eisen's *Children and Play in the Holocaust: Games Among the Shadows*; Rubin Katz's *Gone to Pitchipoï: A Boy's Desperate Fight for Survival in Wartime*; Rochelle G. Saidel's *Mielec, Poland: The Shtetl That Became a Nazi Concentration Camp*; Aviad Kleinberg's article 'The Enchantment of Judaism; Israeli Anxieties and Puzzles,' *Critical Inquiry* 35, no. 3 (spring 2009); Claude Lanzmann's documentary *Shoah*; and Daniel Mendelsohn's *The Lost: A Search for Six of Six Million*.

The book was also inconceivable without the inspiration, support, and expertise provided by Creaghan Trainor, Daniel Mendelsohn, Edan Dekel, Andrea Barrett, Rebecca Ohm, Rich Remsberg, Marketa Rulikova, Dan Polsby, Tomasz Kuznar, and Michael Gross; the saving editorial enthusiasm and intelligence provided by Ben George, Reagan Arthur, Jim Rutman, Peter Matson, and Gary Fisketjon; and the research resources provided by Ron Coleman, Vincent Slatt, Caroline Waddell, and Nancy Hartman of the United States Holocaust Memorial Museum; Theresa Roy of the National Archives; Agnieszka Witkowska-Krych at the Korczakianum Center of Documentation and Research; Agnieszka Reszka of the Żydowski Instytut

Historyczny; Aleksandra Bańkowska and Jan Jagielski at the Emanuel Ringelblum Jewish Historical Institute; and Justyna Majewska at the Museum of the History of Polish Jews. I also have Agnieszka Wojtowicz-Jach and Wojciech Blaszczyk and Monika Oleśko to thank for their help in negotiating Warsaw. And the irrepressible and endlessly informative Alex Dunai to thank for his sheer resourcefulness and expert guidance in both the Polish countryside and the cities.

I also feel enormous humility in the face of the special debt the book owes to the testimonies of Frieda Aaron, Irena Abraham, Fela Abramowicz, Erwin Baum, Israel Berkenwald, Abraham Bomba, Helen Bromberg, Nelly Cesana, Mietek Ejchel, Lily Fenster, Henry Frankel, Simon Friedman, Henry Goldberg, Sam Goldberg, Henia Goldman, Doris Fuchs Greenberg, Marcel Gurner, David Haskil, Josef Himmelblau, Jola Hoffman, David Jakubowski, Erner Jurek, David Kochalski, Andrzej Krauthamer, Sara Lajbowicz, Anne Levy, Anna Lewkowicz, Jakub Michlewicz, Irene and Shimon Noskovicz, Henry Nusbaum, Samuel Offen, Michel Pinkas, Golda Rifka, Anka Rochman, Slama Rotter, Lidia Siciarz, Jack Spiegel, Czerna Sterma, Fela Warschau, Ryszard Weidman, Cyla Wiener, and especially Marian Marzynski.

Finally, I want to single out for special thanks and praise the contributions of those readers who encountered this work in its earliest stages, and whose optimism and rigor helped keep the project afloat: Gary Zebrun, Ron Hansen, and especially Sandra Leong, whose insights, early and late, were a crucial help. And I want most to celebrate my first and final reader, Karen Shepard, who remains fully justified in continuing to inform everyone that she renovates me for the better just about every single day.

Glossary

beshert	destiny
daven	to pray
Judenrat	Jewish administrative council reporting to German occupation
kheyder	religious school run by a rabbi
kishke	intestine stuffed with meat, onion and grain
macher	a fixer — one who gets things done
Ordnungsdienst	Jewish police
peyes	sidelocks worn by hasidic Jews
Seder	ritual meal commemorating the liberation of the Israelites from slavery in ancient Egypt
shlemiel	awkward or unlucky person
shul	synagogue
Talmud-toyres	Jewish community-supported school
treyf	non-kosher
Umschlagplatz	square in Warsaw from

| | which transports to labor and death camps were made |
| Volkesdeutsche | ethnic Germans living outside the Reich but with linguistic and cultural affinity to it |

Other titles published by Ulverscroft:

THE SONG OF THE STORK

Stephan Collishaw

As the Second World War burns through Europe, a fifteen-year-old Jewish girl is on the run in the Polish countryside, having narrowly escaped the German soldiers. Now Yael is alone, with only the memory of her brother Josef — fighting with the Red Army far away — to sustain her. Desperate and determined, she seeks shelter on the farm of the village outcast. Aleksei is mute and solitary, and wary of hiding a Jew. But, as the brutal winter advances, he reluctantly takes her in . . . and a delicate relationship begins to flourish between them in their private sanctuary.

GENERATION

Paula McGrath

1958: A young Irishman, keen to see the world and escape from the back-breaking life of scratching a living from the soil, sets sail for Canada to work in the uranium mines. 2010: Aine, the miner's daughter, worn down by life and single motherhood, leaves Ireland with her daughter Daisy to spend six weeks working on an organic farm in Illinois — and conducting a passionate affair with Joe, the owner. But Joe has secrets to hide, and the revelation of one of them drops a bombshell onto Aine's new life . . .